INTERLIBRARY LOAN

INTERLIBRARY LOAN

GENE WOLFE

TOR

A TOM DOHERTY ASSOCIATES BOOK
NEW YORK

This is a work of fiction. All of the characters, organizations,
and events portrayed in this novel are either products of the author's
imagination or are used fictitiously.

INTERLIBRARY LOAN

A Tor Book
Published by Tom Doherty Associates
120 Broadway
New York, NY 10271

www.tor-forge.com

Tor® is a registered trademark of Macmillan Publishing Group, LLC.

The Library of Congress Cataloging-in-Publication Data
is available upon request.

ISBN 978-1-250-24236-5 (hardcover)
ISBN 978-1-250-24268-6 (ebook)

Our books may be purchased in bulk for promotional, educational, or
business use. Please contact your local bookseller or the Macmillan Corporate
and Premium Sales Department at 1-800-221-7945, extension 5442,
or by email at MacmillanSpecialMarkets@macmillan.com.

First Edition: 2020

Printed in the United States of America

0 9 8 7 6 5 4 3 2 1

INTERLIBRARY LOAN

1

FROM THE SPICE GROVE PUBLIC LIBRARY

In the evening, when the library has closed, the 'bots have locked the big front doors, and everything is quiet, I hear once more the patter of Chandra's black Mary Janes on our white Neostone floor. It seems strange, but now that we're back home I can't stop thinking about Chandra. Or Audrey, whom Chandra called "the lady captain." About the girl I knew once and the woman who had loved and accepted me. What it was like for the three of us on board the *Three Sisters*. How we had looked over the rail sometimes, peering straight down through clear blue water and beholding the ravening monsters of the deep.

Am I or am I not the master of my thoughts? When I choose not to think of those things, my mind fills with thoughts of Dr. Fevre and his brother, and of all the wondrous things Dr. Fevre had accomplished—all of those things and the green box, too. Was he a wizard? I had done a few impossible things myself.

At other times my mind spins with all the thousands of things that happened then. Sometimes I do my best to think only of the good things—of the pure and shining things, because I know that destiny and the world are not all dark. Love is more real than the longest river, and kindness means more than any mountain range.

When I have finished deciding on all the thousand things I can never forget about Colette Coldbrook and the crude little mine that circles some other star, I promised myself I would never write about anything like that again. No! Not ever again! Because it hurts too much and tears my soul to shreds when I strive to think back on all those things: Audrey, the boundless sea, Cadaver Island, Buck Baston, the dead girls, and all the rest. Now I cannot banish those things from my thoughts. The high, empty, echoing, haunted house at the top of the hill and all the rest of it. The click of high, hard heels in another room on another floor. Now it seems to me that writing down all the most important events here may help me clear my mind and let me think instead of the little empty things going on in this unmeaning museum now. Things over and done with when I have finished. If I ever do.

Or anyway I dare to hope that this writing may.

Now where to start? What would you like to read about, dear unborn fully human patron, and what must you read about first if you are to understand the rest? Perhaps I should begin when we left—but just a day or two before that might be better. Too soon a start outshines too late, or at least so it seems to me. If I should begin a bit too soon, please leave a note in this manuscript advising any future readers to skip my soft, overripe beginning and jump to the true beginning as you would yourself if you were ever to read all this again—instructing your future self to begin to read on page whatever when all the dull machinery of importance has been set in motion.

So I'm going to go way far back and start my story where I want to, with graceful Rose and my friend Millie.

Millie Baumgartner is like me, a reclone resource here in the Spice Grove Public Library; and I'm sure she looks quite a bit older than she really is. Gray streaks in her lustrous brown hair, lines in her face, and a little too plump; but she has a wonderful smile that she was not using when she came up to me and whispered, "They're going to get rid of us, Ern. Have you heard?"

The Fire did not seem likely so soon for either of us; so I shook my head, more than a little bit puzzled.

"We're going east in a beautiful new truck. Brand new and really elegant."

I stopped myself from saying, "Huh?" and shut my mouth instead.

"The new truck means the Continental Library. They say that's where it goes."

I said, "If they were going to burn us, they could do it in the incinerator here, Millie. You know they could."

She did not say a word, so after I'd given her a good chance to, I went back to talking. "You wrote all those wonderful cookbooks. Sometimes it seems like you get checked out three times a week."

That made her smile, honest and warm. "You're a sweet boy, Ern. Thank you."

"I doubt it. Truthful, though." I've got to talk like that, just in case you're wondering. I have to talk exactly like the exposition in the first Ern A. Smithe's books, whether I like it or not. My brain was hardwired for it from the beginning, and I cannot do one damned thing about it no matter how much it embarrasses me.

"I'm a terrible troublemaker, Ern. I criticize the groceries and the cooking. Sometimes I go into the kitchen and try to teach the cooks how to make a tossed salad. They don't like it one little bit."

That must have made me smile. "They should be grateful."

"Yes indeed. And everybody everywhere ought to be a whole lot nicer, but saying so doesn't help."

I agreed but couldn't keep from grinning.

Millie tapped my chest with her index finger. "You're a troublemaker, too, Ern. You're a big one."

Pure as snow I declared that I tried not to be.

"Well you are, just the same." Her plump finger tapped my chest again. "Shall I list all your faults?"

I just about laughed at that one. "Dinner's in another hour, and you'll need a lot more time."

"Later, maybe." Millie sighed and started over. "It's you and me and Rose." By that time I had noticed her orange tag. Now she held it up. "A 'bot's looking for you right this minute with one of these. It says 'AA twenty-three.' AA means the new truck."

It did, and the orange tag also meant interlibrary loan. Those numbers on the tag told the 'bots which truck to which library; it seemed to me that for Continental the number ought to have been one, but that was not what was on our tags. It should have tipped me off right away, but I wasn't sharp enough to get it.

About an hour later they handed out navy-blue winter coats and put the three of us in the truck—that was Millie, Rose

Romain the romance writer, and me. When I had ridden in one of those trucks before, interlibrary loan had meant sitting on stacks of books in the back, and it had been bumpy and too dark to read back there. This was way better than that. Just to start, we were not really riding in the truck. The truck pulled a couple of big trailers, and we were in the second one. There were about two hundred disks, cubes, and real old-fashioned books with pages in it with us; but it was specially fitted out for reclones like the three of us, for breathing, bleeding library resources who didn't count as fully humans and could be torn to pieces by angry patrons pretty much at will. Read my first book if you don't understand. It's here too.

Now back to the truck and its trailers.

The biggest plus of all was that our trailer was adequately heated. Another big, big plus was plumbing; there was a chemical toilet with a green curtain around it, and a washbasin, far better than a bucket of water and a hole in the floor.

There were narrow fold-up bunks on both sides, too; upper and lower bunks, not cushy but almost as good as the soft, self-heated mats we slept on in the library. These bunks were, as Millie put it, actual beds that you could fall out of. By fully human standards that trailer was crowded and uncomfortable; but I remembered the truck I had ridden in when Owenbright sent me back to Spice Grove, and this one was a long ton better.

Up there I should have mentioned that there were lights inside, too, bright bottled sunshine we could turn on and off; and there were strong primary colors all over, red and blue mostly. But the main thing as far as I was concerned was that there were windows. I had expected no windows, and if somebody had told me there would be windows, I would have expected notint. These were variables, which gave us a fine opportunity to argue about which ones should be light and which ones dark, and which of the dark ones were too dark or not dark enough. You know.

Millie and I wanted all of them pretty clear, and Rose wanted all of them black, so nobody could stare at her and maybe make finger signs. Rose was a redhead, ghost-pale and slender only at the waist; she looked to be about twenty. How old she was really I have no idea. (With reclones like the three of us you can never know for sure, because what if we're not telling you the truth?) Millie looked about fifty, and my guess was thirty or forty. Rose? Who the hell knew? She had to have a shelf right next to the floor, meaning a Number One because she said men—meaning me—would try to look up her skirt if she had to climb a ladder. Listening to her argue about that with the 'bots and cry at the librarians, I got to where I would have tried it just to keep her happy. If you've been wondering why Millie called Rose a troublemaker, now you know.

So three troublemakers on their way to Continental, or at least that's what we thought. Did we make lots of trouble for each other on the truck? You bet we did! If I was to tell you all about it, all the loud two-way quarrels and all the louder three-way arguments, you'd laugh yourself sick.

Here's an example. Millie wanted nice clear windows so she could reread her own cookbooks and look through the old magazines for a recipe column she had written way back when.

I wanted them clear, too. For me it was because I wanted to see out. Sure, I liked seeing the wide, wintry plain, the pine woods full of flying snow, and all the icy rivers and haunted ruins just like other people; but there was more to it than that. When you feel like you've spent your whole life in the Twenty-first Century and all of a sudden you get reprinted and find yourself up where I did, you can't help trying to get your bearings—or anyhow I can't. I've never been able to figure out where Saint Louis used to be; but I'm pretty sure the big snow-capped mountains Arabella and I had flown over to look at one time used to be the Rockies. I had a notion that Spice Grove would have been somewhere in Nebraska, but that could have been wrong. It could have been in the Dakotas instead, or even someplace up around Winnipeg.

Anyway, the mountains were the best part. The worst part was the old-time city, with torn-up streets branching off the highway, a few ragged kids, and a lot of empty buildings. I liked those every bit as much as Rose liked Millie's cookbooks.

So the argument was two against one, and so easy I felt kind of guilty about it. When it was over Rose sat on her bunk with a blanket covering her lap and those long, smooth legs, put her hands over her tits, and pouted; and Millie and I felt bad enough to turn the window across from her full dark. The other three we left as clear as notint.

Every so often I tried to quiz Millie about Niagara, where it was and why they called it that, and how it had gotten to be the capital of the continent. She did not know much more than I did, but she reminded me that the falls move. Falls are really just water pouring over a cliff, and as time passes they wear away their cliff so that stones and gravel fall down it with the water. Rock by rock, the falls creep upstream.

So that was bad and there was more. In my time, only a little bit of the water really poured over the falls at Niagara; the rest was tapped off to drive turbines and generate electricity.

All that was nuclear now, so there would be a lot more water going over, enough to change things pretty fast. Was this Niagara what we called Niagara Falls, New York, back when I was born? Or else Niagara Falls, Canada? Was it both? Maybe, but maybe not. So when I got a good opening I tried asking Millie a whole bunch of questions, starting with, "Why do you think they want us?"

That first one made her laugh. "You think they want us just because they're getting us?"

I held up my orange tag. "Interlibrary loan, right? They must have asked for us."

"They didn't. That's what my source said."

That raised my eyebrows. "It sounds like you've been talking to a librarian. I'll keep quiet about it, and you'd better keep quiet, too."

"Suppose I told you that a bunch of us, six reference reclones and four librarians, sit around together to sew a quilt, Ern? You know, in Handicrafts after the rest of you have turned in. Naturally we chat while we stitch. Want to look at the place where I stuck my finger with the needle last night? I jumped when Eloise told me that Continental was desperate to get me, and that's when I stabbed myself. I was attempting suicide."

She was kidding about the suicide and desperation. I knew it, and she knew I knew it; so I said, "They didn't ask for us?"

Rose looked up. "They don't need us and wouldn't want us. Continental has dozens of copies of everybody."

"Spice Grove would like to get rid of us," Millie said. "I told you that."

"Sure. They'd burn us tomorrow if they had the guts. We're troublemakers."

"Only Spice Grove can't do that, because there would be too many questions. You were right about me—I get checked out almost as much as I'd like to be, just to start with. There would be pressure to get another copy, maybe quite a lot of it."

I nodded.

"Rose not as much. For her it's five or six times a year, I think. But still . . ." She let it hang.

"Sure. That's quite a bit more than I do."

"It is, but that girl who checks you out every year has connections and a ton of money. Besides, she used to be a teacher here."

She meant Colette Coldbrook. I said, "Sure, but it was in a private school."

"In a posh prep school. That gives her more pull, not less. She'd have questions, her influential friends would have questions, and what could they say?"

I had thought of something. "If they wanted to get rid of us, they wouldn't have to burn us. They could just offer all three of us for sale."

"It might be months before we sold, Ern; and one or two of us might never sell at any price. This works right away. We're gone, aren't we?" Millie took a deep breath.

I could see she was afraid the driver would overhear her. There was a gadget in our trailer that we could switch on anytime we wanted to talk to him. We kept it turned off, but did the OFF position really prevent him from overhearing what we said? For all we knew it could be on all the time. I doubted that he would worry a lot about what three reclones were saying (or even four, because there were four bunks), but you never know. Somebody with a lot of clout might *want* him to be worried about it and write a report after the run.

"What they're doing now gets rid of us for a while, and if they're lucky it will get rid of us forever. They tag us for inter-library loan and send us off to Continental. Spice Grove has less than twenty reclones."

I nodded. Before we left there had been eighteen.

"Continental will have hundreds. Thousands, maybe. I've no idea what its budget is, but it must be incredible. Half a billion a year or even more. So what do they care about three more reclones, three reclones they don't even have to pay for? From what I've heard, there are a hundred million titles on Continental's shelves. The bureaucracy must be enormous."

Millie warmed to her subject. "It could be years before some-body realizes that they never asked for us and sends us back. Years or decades, even though they've probably got dozens and dozens of copies of all three of us already."

I said, "A couple dozen of you, anyway."

"And dozens and dozens of me," Rose put in.

No way was I sure of that and I doubt that Rose was either, but I said, "Right. One hell of a lot of you both." Anything to keep the peace.

Outside our trailer, snowbanks, leafless trees, and snow-covered ruins—plus fully humans wearing what were probably heated hats and mufflers—flashed by. Especially leafless trees. There were a heck of a lot more trees than fully humans and their farmhouses put together. I had a good many more questions for Millie; but they were not all that interesting, my questions or her answers either. I'll skip those.

Miles, kilometers, and furlongs down that lonely, winding road our truck finally pulled in someplace for the night. Stop-ping for the night meant supper for everybody and a nice warm room close by for the driver. As I may have mentioned, I still had quite a bit of the money I'd taken from Colette Coldbrook's shaping bag; but I kept it in my pocket, feeling pretty certain I would need it later.

So all three of us ate the supper the driver bought for us, which meant a cup of chicken noodle and a club sandwich on white toast. I told him he didn't have to take us back to our trailer, we would take care of it ourselves. No deal on that—he marched the three of us back and locked us in.

It was pretty dark in there with the lights off and all four windows dialed to BLACK; but undressing was a problem anyway, one that all of us had most likely seen coming. I undressed first, telling the ladies they could look if they wanted to. I don't think either of them did. After that, I climbed into one of the top bunks and turned my face toward the wall. In the morning I found out that Rose had slept in her clothes; it was something I ought to have seen coming, but I had not. That much modesty in one of us seemed pretty silly.

We got to Niagara the next day. I already knew that most of the Continental Library was underground in tunnels and big shadowy underground rooms that were almost three hundred years old; so I expected only a small building up on the surface. Wrong! It was huge, the pale stone nightmare of somebody who had seen the pyramids once, and it had too many levels for me to count before we rolled inside. We stopped; before long our driver unlocked our door and all three of us got out. What happened next was simple, quick, and quiet—and it caught me flatfooted.

He locked it behind us. I had not been expecting to get back in, and I do not think Millie or Rose had either; so it struck me as kind of strange. He, or more likely his boss, thought we might try to get away from something.

Pretty soon after that, one of the 'bots who had been unloading the truck and the first trailer came over and said, "Come with me." Then it herded the three of us ahead of it the way they do, arms extended and spread wide. We hiked down rough corridors without windows for an hour or so, with me wondering where the hell we were going. When we finally got there, I shouldn't have been surprised, but I was.

The 'bot put us into another truck parked in another part of the building, a truck that was smaller and quite a bit older than ours had been, and nearly empty. Later I counted the books and disks in there with us: seventeen. So fewer than two dozen books and disks, two or three cubes, a slop bucket, and the three of us reclone resources.

Do I have to tell you we were locked in? We were, of course. That wasn't too bad, but we'd left our coats back in the trailer. All three of us had, and I imagine the women felt as dumb about that as I did. When our new truck (which was really a pretty old one) began rolling, I stared at them and the two of them stared back at me. After a while Rose managed to say, "I imagine we're going home to Spice Grove." She tried to smile.

Millie held up her tag. It was dark in the back of the truck, but not too dark for me to see that. She said, "They would have given us new tags."

So this was planned from the beginning. No truck ran from Spice Grove to wherever we were going, but there was one to Continental. So ship us off to Continental, and they would put us on the right truck for wherever it was that we were wanted.

That was Polly's Cove, as it turned out. I'll have quite a bit more to say about Polly's Cove later.

All right, I was getting ahead of myself; but there is not much more to tell. Our truck went to various libraries and unloaded a few books and disks and so forth, and loaded a few new ones at each of them. When we finally stopped for the first night, I was able to talk the driver into letting me buy us blankets. Coats would have been better, but nice warm coats for all three of us would have cost twice what I had. Blankets were cheaper, and I could afford three of them. It left me a little over, but not much. A blanket—even a cheap one—is pretty warm if you wrap yourself up in it.

By the third night I felt like we were never going to get wherever we were going; the libraries would just ship us here and there until we wore out or went crazy. We reclone resources do go crazy pretty often, but most of us had been writers the first time around; the rest had been artists, nearly all of them. With writers it can be hard to tell, and with artists it is next to impossible.

When we got out of the truck, we did not even know we were about to walk into the Polly's Cove Public Library. We were a mess, all three of us, with dirty faces and dirty, wrinkled clothes. Millie apologized to the head librarian for the way we looked, and Rose and I tried to explain. While we talked, the head librarian stared at us without saying a word; to tell the truth I was not sure she had understood anything any of us said.

When she had gone, I looked at Millie and she looked at me. I said, "I guess she speaks French." I was trying to be witty.

"She didn't look French." That was Rose.

It made me think of Georges; I smiled and shut up, and wished to God that Georges were there with us.

Later we found out that the head librarian was stone deaf. She had been reading lips and had not talked because she knew she was hard for strangers to understand. We saw more of her after that than we wanted to, so I might as well tell you that she was taller than I am and as thin as a rake. She wore a lot of black and had dyed black hair. Her name was Prentice. Probably she had a first name, too; but I don't think I ever heard it. I don't know about you, so maybe you're like me. Do you wonder sometimes about people like Prentice? Had she ever been in love, ever had a child, ever played on a jumpball team? All librarians read, but what kind of books did Prentice like?

I was still thinking about that stuff when she left and another librarian, blond, pretty, and at least thirty years younger, came in and introduced herself; this one's name was Charlotte Lang. I said something about being glad to find a librarian we could talk to, and she said, "Oh, I'm not a real librarian, Mr. Smithe. I only work here part-time. I'm just a volunteer, but Ms. Prentice said for me to look after you."

Of course she had made two mistakes right from the start. For one thing, a part-time librarian is a real librarian, just part-time. The other was that instead of calling me "Smithe," she had called me "Mr. Smithe." The librarians are not supposed to do that. So two mistakes, and I liked her for both of them. So I gave her my nicest smile and introduced Rose and Millie.

"Oh, I'm so glad you're here, Ms. Baumgartner! I asked for you, and Ms. Prentice finally got you. She said she couldn't buy us a copy—we don't have nearly enough money for that—but she promised she'd borrow one. She said she could get you from the big library in Niagara or someplace like that."

Millie started to say something then, but Charlotte wasn't through. "And you, Ms. Romain! I read you all the time before I got married, only now I read Ms. Baumgartner more because I'm not a very good cook, not really half as good as my mother even, and I've learned ever so much from reading Ms. Baumgartner. The library has *The Pleasures of Pork* and *Game Can Be Fun.* Well, really I'm reading that one now. I've finished reading 'Duck and Goose,' and I'm halfway through 'Pheasant Can Be Pleasant.' That's Chapter Four, isn't it?"

Millie agreed that it was.

"People liked my duck, too. I had to use chili powder instead of allspice and I didn't care for it much myself, but Bub and his friend said it was good—great is what they said—and your roast pheasant with chestnuts! Oh, my! It was perfectly scrumptious."

Millie smiled and said, "That wasn't my roast pheasant you enjoyed so much, Ms. Lang. It was yours."

Charlotte actually blushed. "Well, you—you'll want baths, I know. Everybody will. Baths and clean clothes. I'm afraid only one can bathe at a time here; it's all we've got facilities for, so you'll have to take turns. I'll be fetching your clean things while you're washing. Would you like to go first, Ms. Baumgartner? Will that be all right with everybody?"

Naturally I nodded and said sure; I suppose Rose did, too. After that Rose and I sat and waited, me wishing that I could have a quiet look around and get the layout of the library, but knowing it was way too early for me to make any kind of trouble—and snooping around would probably turn out to be big trouble if Prentice caught me. After ten minutes or so, Charlotte came back with a short stack of clean clothes for me, but I didn't want to strip and put them on with Rose sitting there. Besides the embarrassment, I was grimy and sweaty from the truck. That library was worse if anything, dusty and overheated and then some.

When Millie came out and Rose went in, Millie wanted to know if I had met some of the other reclones. I said no, I hadn't even seen them.

"Have you had a look at the shelves? They must have shelves for us or they wouldn't have borrowed us."

I shook my head. "I've been right here the whole time. How do you like your new clothes?"

"I want an apron. If I can get a good one, the rest will do." Millie clammed up for a bit, maybe because my watch was striking; then she said, "You can hold the fort until Rose comes out, but I'm going to sneak around."

The idea of Millie sneaking around just about made me laugh. Millie would have made some country a terrific spy, because nobody would ever suspect her of anything. I said, "I'll sneak along with you. Rose is good for a solid hour. Maybe more."

Our bathroom opened on the dusty little hall I had already walked down behind Charlotte. I pointed to the way we had come and told Millie to go that way. I would go the other way and have a look. After that we'd meet back in the bathroom and compare notes. Ten or twelve strides brought me to the end of the hall, and a door there opened on a good-sized room with high shelves and a lot of empty space. There were more shelves on the other side of them. No labels on anything anywhere, but opening a couple of the books told me I was in History. Maybe Ancient History, because that was what all the books I looked at seemed to be about: Ancient Greece or Egypt or Babylon. Those books were pretty ancient themselves. The paper was yellowing, and somebody had made notes in the margins of one, in neat cursive. Cursive made it a hundred and fifty years old, minimum. Probably quite a bit more.

So another tall case, this one almost entirely empty. Which was good, because looking between its empty shelves I saw something I had not seen since I died the first time. It was an iron staircase of piece-of-pie-shaped steps coiled tight around an iron pole.

The History Room—I could see everything in it as soon as I had climbed up the first half dozen steps—was even smaller than I had thought. It had a nice high ceiling, though, and a couple of tall windows that would have been a whole lot more interesting if they had not been blocked by tall bookcases.

Upstairs was what they probably called the Stacks. That's where you keep the stuff that patrons cannot just walk up to and pull off the shelf. Here, though, there were no shelves but actual stacks of books and disks and cubes and whatever, some stacked on a couple of tables and the rest on the floor. At the moment none of those things interested me. What did were the windows, two again; tall, narrow, dirty notint windows. Looking out I saw the roofs, roofs of red or brown tile, of what might have been houses or shops.

And way out on the other side of those red and brown roofs, boats.

2

WHAT THE SHIRT SHOWED

Three of them looked like fishing boats, and there were four or five sloops (rich men's toys) bored but resigned to it. All these were moored. Beyond them stretched an ocean of seawater that looked like it went clear around the planet. Just empty salt water, and more salt water, and nothing else; seawater in smooth dark swells as far as my eyes could see. Featureless seawater that looked as smooth as olive oil, and wheeling, moaning seagulls, all under the great curved dome of a clear blue sky without a single cloud. I ought to have looked out at all that for a minute or two, seen what was to be seen, and gone back to my own part of the library. I ought to have, but I didn't. The boats, the gulls, and most of all the water seemed to be telling me that there was a thousand times more to life than I had ever supposed, ten thousand times more to life than being treated like a thing, just a library resource, another battered book standing idle on one of a million slightly dusty library shelves. So I looked and looked and drank it all in, feeling that I could never be just another bipedal book again. The sea and the sky spoke slowly; but in quiet chorus they told me about life, warmth, friendship, and love. Told me in tones that kept me standing there until my legs ached, tired and stiff, spellbound while I drank in all that they had to say.

When I got back to the third-rate restroom where Millie and I were supposed to be waiting for Rose to get out of the tub, Millie was already there. She looked troubled, but she managed a nice friendly smile for me. So I smiled back and made my smile as friendly as I could.

"I found out where we are, Ern." Millie hesitated. "Do we care?"

It was a slippery question the way I felt just then, but I kept my smile while I told her I did.

"This is Polly's Cove." She paused, waiting for some reaction she didn't get. "I've been talking to a patron, a nice kid named Chandra." Millie drew a deep breath. "All right, I know we're not supposed to talk to patrons unless they're consulting us. But under the circumstances it seemed to me that it was time to . . . well, you know. Do something."

I tried to say *sure*, but what came out was "Certainly." Like I told you, I have to talk like that. Pretty often it sucks, but I can't help it.

"Chandra has been looking through all the cookbooks." Millie hesitated again, then decided to back up a little bit. "I had turned up the ones she needed, but there's no copy of *Game Can Be Fun*. What I mean is that there's none shelved—a screen told me it's out. Do you think that was mean of me? Checking up on a nice young part-time librarian like that?"

"Hell no. You wanted to see if Charlotte Lang had told you the truth."

Millie nodded. "And to help this Chandra along, Ern. Besides, I couldn't remember what came after pheasant. That's the last of the game birds, actually. She'd skipped duck, goose, woodcock, and quail. Venison comes next."

I nodded. It seemed clear that the person Chandra was cooking for hunted, and I thought of the deer rifle I'd found in Conrad Coldbrook's mine. It had been a swell gun, but it was gone forever now, and all of a sudden I missed it a lot.

Still remembering, I choked down five or ten minutes worth of stuff I was itching to tell Millie about that gun and substituted, "Rose isn't through yet?"

Rose's voice came from behind the curtain. "I'll be out soon. Just a minute."

Millie told her there was no need to hurry, one of the few times I was tempted to yell at Millie.

It was another half hour at least. Neither of us went out again; but Millie told me various things she had found out about Chandra, and that Chandra had told her the name of the town. I was still not feeling too friendly toward Millie; even so I told her a little bit about the stacks of Ancient History and the tall windows, and what I had seen out of those windows.

When I had finished, Millie said, "There was one other thing I should have told you. You're going to think I'm a liar, but it would be another kind of lie—a really wrong, really terrible lie—not to tell you."

She quit talking then, and I could see she was hoping I'd talk and change the subject. I didn't, and finally she whispered, "I saw a little girl in a white dress, Ern. This wasn't Chandra."

I nodded, trying to make her think I was interested when I really wasn't.

"She was white, too. Her face was paler than her dress, actually. She watched me for a minute, and then she turned away and melted into the wall."

I didn't know what to say. I think I may have said something silly like "wow."

"I can't prove it and you don't have to believe it, but that's what I saw."

Neither of us said anything after that, sitting side by side on a bench and each wrapped in our own thoughts. I was pretty sure somebody had slipped Millie some kind of dope, but who would do that? Who could have done it, and why? Either dope or she was cracking up, and why would she crack up when she wasn't under all that much pressure? I kicked both of those around for quite a while.

Then Rose came out, all fresh and smiling, and looking a lot more like a romance writer in a sleeveless red dress that was almost as low-necked as she liked them and might have been next to new. Have I said that they get our clothes from those places that take clothes donations and give the money to charity when they sell them? Those are dead people's clothes, mostly, and for a minute or two I wondered about the woman who had worn the red dress first.

After that I went in, carrying the clean underwear, the socks, the blue canvas jeans, and a sturdy work shirt that would soon be mine. There had been a clean jacket, too, a quilted black jacket that looked pretty warm; that had been on a hanger. When we came into the room with the curtained tub, Charlotte Lang had taken it off the hanger and hung it on a nail. I had left it there, knowing I could get it when I came out.

Meanwhile, here was a nice clean bathtub with no ring

around it (Rose must have scrubbed that off), a thin old wash-cloth with a hole in it, a little cake of dark yellow soap, and what seemed to be plenty of hot water. I filled the tub as high as I dared and got in, feeling as though I could have stayed right there in the tub for the rest of my life.

There are places to plan and places to dream. Probably you've noticed that yourself. Behind a desk is a place to plan, and so is a seat in just about any kind of a vehicle. The places to dream all begin with B—bed, bar, boudoir, and bathtub. "B" for bemused.

When I finally got out, I found that the ladies had left me one dry towel, just one and no more, a thin towel and pretty small. I could have used three of those, but I poached a little on the ones that they had used and dropped into the laundry bin. I found three or four that were barely damp.

Then it was time for striped cotton (?) undershorts and black socks, with all of them going on smoothly. When I unfolded the work shirt—yellow torso and blue sleeves—I found two shiny metal rectangles on the coarse cloth. There was one well down on the right sleeve, and another on the left side of the torso. Touch one to the other and they stuck together like glue; you had to pull them apart, which was not easy. I tore a fingernail, swore, and tried to pull off the one on the yellow fabric, but they stuck so hard I had to give up on that. Pretty soon I figured out what they were there for.

It was not until I was dressed and looked myself over in the foggy old mirror that I noticed some faint stains. My shirt had been washed and probably bleached, too, and that had weakened them; but they were still there. Small bloodstains up near the right shoulder.

3

THE HOUSE ON SIGNAL HILL

The reclone section was in nonfiction, which was fine for Millie but wrong for Rose and me. The ponticwood shelves here were four high, just as they were in Spice Grove; but that was where all resemblance ended. Here there were no washbasins and no curtained toilets—no plumbing of any kind on the shelves. There were beds, but they were no wider than graves and not much thicker than our old mats. These beds had reading lights on the headboards; that was about it. No sitting down in a red leather chair with a nice floor lamp for reading; if we wanted to sit down, we sat on the bed or on the shelf, cross-legged or with our legs hanging over. If we had to go, Millie from her two and I from my three climbed down the ladder and went back to the restroom we'd been in before. Bathing, the same. Patrons used that restroom, too; it wasn't just for us. Librarians had their own (I found out later) across the hall from Prentice's office. They had to get the key from her and give it back as soon as they were finished. If one of us asked for that key, she threw her stapler or the kafe cup from her desk. I know because I had to duck them both.

So that was Polly's Cove except for the food, which came as a happy shock to all three of us—it was one hell of a lot better than Spice Grove's. We got lobster that first night, half of a big broiled lobster for each of us. Fish chowder came first; and our lobsters brought along corn on the cob, a baked potato, and a first-rate salad. Salad at Spice Grove had been chopped lettuce splashed with vinegar and oil; in Polly's Cove it was tender young spinach with chopped red onions, cheddar, and country ham mixed in. Your choice of Thousand Island or ranch. Millie and I chose Thousand Island, and happily. So good food, and good food makes a big difference.

What's more, I surprised the living hell out of Rose, Millie, and everybody else at the library (very much including me) by getting checked out on the third day.

If I said "girl," it would sound like nineteen or twenty with curves and makeup, right? So I won't. Let's call her a kid. The first time I was with her I figured her for twelve. Later I found out she was almost thirteen, so I had been right but close to wrong. She told me her name was Chandra, but at first I didn't make the connection.

"I have to bring you home to my mother, Mr. Smithe. I'll tell you all about that after I check you out, or else my mother will."

Still looking down at her from my shelf, I shook my head. "You would need to put up a great deal of money to check me out, Chandra. I'm sure you don't have that much."

"I'll talk to them, Mr. Smithe. Come with me."

"If you want to talk to me, you can do it right here. That way you won't need any money."

This time Chandra shook her head, making her brown braids bounce. "I'd have to come back for you, probably with a librarian or you wouldn't come."

"That's right." I can be as dumb as anybody, but as soon as I said that it soaked through to me that if I jumped off my shelf and went to the desk with this kid it might count as being consulted. Sure, consulted was not nearly as good as being checked out, but it was a lot better than nothing. When the Polly's Cove Library returned us to Spice Grove, it would report how many checkouts we'd had, and how many consultations. You did not throw away a consultation. Millie Baumgartner might do that, but not Ern A. Smithe.

So off we went to the desk—that's me and a pretty, brown-haired girl who came up almost to my chin. Charlotte Lang was on the desk. She smiled at both of us and said hello to Chandra.

"I have to check him out," Chandra explained. "Mother wants to talk to him, so I promised I'd check him out for her."

Charlotte said, "I'm afraid I'll have to speak with her."

Chandra nodded and started giving her mother's address, but Charlotte said she didn't need it, and turned to her screen. I would like to have seen the picture when she got her party, but of course I couldn't. The screen was angled so somebody on the wrong side of the desk couldn't see it. They always are.

Charlotte said, "Your daughter says you want to check out our new copy of Ern A. Smithe, Mrs. Fevre. Checking out a reclone resource requires a large deposit, returned when you return the reclone on time. I'm sure you know."

I couldn't hear the reply.

"When you return it on time and undamaged. In good condition. Otherwise . . ."

—

"We still have that older copy, you understand. We're selling it now, and it's very inexpensive."

—

"Fine. I'll send him along with Chandra. They should be with you soon."

Charlotte Lang touched the sign-off and turned back to us. "Your mother says you're to come straight home. No side trips and no dawdling." To me, "I doubt that you know where the house is, Smithe. Do you?"

I shook my head. "I have no idea."

"Turn left as you go out. Signal Hill Road will be the third street, I believe. Left again on that. It's a three-story white neo-Goth house all the way up the hill, with a widow's walk. You can't miss it."

Chandra said, "Besides, you'll have me with you."

Charlotte nodded. "I certainly hope so."

There was an old man sitting in the little reception room next to a heap of discards. He was staring at the floor and did not look up as we passed. At the time, I failed to connect him with anything Charlotte had said.

When we had turned onto Signal Hill Road, Charlotte wanted to know if I had money.

"A little," I told her. "Not very much."

She nodded thoughtfully.

We walked on in silence for half a block before she asked, "Would you like to get some more?"

"Not if the library is to know I have it."

Chandra nodded again. "It's the same way with me sometimes. Will you buy me a steaming creamy?" She pointed. "That's a candy store up ahead."

"I take it they sell steaming creamys." I had no idea what a steaming creamy was.

She nodded solemnly.

"If I buy you one, will your mother approve?"

"That's the other thing. You mustn't tell her."

"Then I won't."

"You'll buy it for me? Please? Just a small one."

"All right, just a small one. What flavor?"

"Cantaloupe custard." Chandra took my hand. "That's my fave."

"Got it." I paused, considering. "If I buy you the steaming creamy, will you tell me what your mother wants with me?"

Chandra looked troubled. "I don't know a lot—not for sure."

"What you think, in that case."

She thought that over for three or four steps before saying, "All right. What I think."

Seeing Chandra, the woman behind the counter in the candy store said, "One cantaloupe custard, coming up!"

I nodded and added, "A small one. Chocolate for me, a small one."

Chandra looked slightly alarmed. "Don't get it on your shirt."

I said, "This shirt has bloodstains on it already. What's a little chocolate compared to that?"

"Mother will know."

"I'll tell her I was going to buy you a steaming creamy too, but you said you weren't permitted to accept it."

"Really?"

I nodded. "Yes. Really."

Chandra accepted her cup. "You know, I like you."

I accepted my chocolate one. "Then you'll tell me what you think, just as you promised."

She nodded and started for the door.

I paid and sipped before following her.

"You won't tell anybody what I told you?"

"No, since you don't want me to."

"All right. Mother thinks somebody's trying to kill her. Mostly it's with magic, but sometimes it's with other things, too. There's a black thing—"

"Wait up. Why would anyone want to kill her?"

"I think it's something about the accident." Chandra seemed plainly troubled. "Mother was in an accident when I was real young. Some kind of accident or something on a boat. It's why she hardly ever gets out of bed."

That sounded like paranoia and set me wondering.

"There's things hiding in the house, too. That's why she keeps the lights on all night."

"I see."

"I've got a room of my own, but I've got to sleep with Mother, so there's somebody else there."

"And the lights must make it hard to sleep."

"Not really. You just shut your eyes and keep them shut. Sometimes the electricity goes off, but we have lanterns, too. I get up and light two for us."

"Do you think there are really things hiding in your house?"

Chandra nodded solemnly.

"What makes you think that?"

"One comes into the bedroom sometimes, late at night. It

creeps in, flat on the floor." She paused. "Sometimes it cries. It says, 'No bite.'"

"Really?" I had almost forgotten my chocolate steaming creamy; now I gave it a well-deserved sip, wondering whether there was a word of truth in anything Chandra had said. Was this nice kid stringing me? Or stringing herself?

"You've seen it?" I was trying to sound skeptical; it didn't take a lot of effort.

"Kind of. It's big and black and makes scratchy noises and lies really flat against the floor. That makes it hard to see when it's dark in there."

"But it talks and cries. You said that."

"Uh-huh. Little words and little crying noises." Chandra paused, giving her attention to her steaming creamy. "This is really good."

I nodded. "And this is a really good story you're telling me; the question is whether it's a really true story."

"You didn't say true, you said what I think."

"You think a black thing crawls into your mother's room late at night."

Looking very serious, she nodded. "I've seen it."

"What do you do when that happens?"

"I yell at it to get out. Sometimes I throw shoes or bottles. Whatever's handy."

"Yelling must wake up your mother."

Chandra nodded. "It does. She screams and screams. Then the black thing runs away."

"Out the door?"

That took thought. "Sort of out the door or something. It goes away."

"Sort of out the door?"

"It can be hard to tell. It could be out the other door or out a window. Maybe into the closet."

When I said nothing she added, "Will you sleep with my mother tonight instead of me? Maybe you can see it."

I considered that one. "You sleep in her bed, in bed with her?"

Chandra nodded.

"I can't do that, it's against the rules. I have to sleep on the floor next to her bed."

"I'd like to sleep in my own room sometimes."

"I understand, and I will be proud to sleep on the floor beside a fully human's bed."

About that time I spotted the three-story white house with the widow's walk. "I'd like to propose a theory for your consideration. It seems to me that your mother may suffer from paranoid schizophrenia. It's not uncommon for schizophrenics—paranoid schizophrenics, particularly—to infect other members of their immediate family. Those so infected are not actually schizophrenic and often recover quickly when separated from the true paranoid schizophrenic. But they come to believe the schizophrenic's delusions until such separation occurs."

"You think my mother's crazy, and she's made me crazy, too."

"I'm asking you if it isn't possible." I shivered, wishing that gloves and a heated cap had come with my new jacket.

"The black thing's really there. I see it almost every night." Chandra sounded sure of her ground.

"Really there, but you can't see how it gets in?"

Chandra shook her head.

"Surely you must see how it gets out."

"It just goes away. It isn't there anymore." Chandra paused, and audibly swallowed. "It sort of fades into the dark."

Like a dream, I thought. It seemed impolite to say it aloud, so I didn't.

Chandra's mother's bedroom was on the ground floor, with two narrow, snow-dotted windows looking out and down the other side of the long slope that Chandra and I had just climbed. "Please take a chair, Mr. Smithe." There was a spindly, armless chair near the bed. I sat down on it gingerly, trying to keep from staring at the big, dark eyes and high cheekbones of the white-faced woman between the sheets.

"You are newly come to our village library, Mr. Smithe? That's what Chandra tells me."

"Correct. We got here yesterday, Millie Baumgartner"—the pale woman in the big bed tried to wave the name away—"Rose Romain, and I," I finished.

"You know nothing of Polly's Cove?"

"Correct. I have never been here before, and I had never heard of it."

"That's unfortunate. On the other hand, a new man, a younger man . . ."

"As is often the case. I take it you didn't check me out in order to quiz me about my books."

The pale woman spoke to Chandra. "Please leave us, darling. Ask Mrs. Heuse to make you something for lunch."

When the door had shut behind Chandra, her mother said, "I would prefer to question you about a book of mine." She indicated a large leather-bound volume on her bedside table. "Look inside the back cover, please."

It was a map, dotted with symbols I did not recognize.

I said, "May I carry this to the window?"

She nodded. "As long as you don't leave it there."

"I won't."

The big book was even heavier than I had expected, but I rested the top on the windowsill. When I had finished looking, I closed its faded black leather cover and brought it back to the little bedside table.

The pale woman opened her eyes. "You were thorough, Mr. Smithe. I like that."

"Not really. You know my name and I ought to have learned yours from Chandra, but I didn't. May I ask it now?"

For the first time, she smiled.

"You looked at the bookplate in front. I saw that."

"I did, and I felt certain it wasn't yours. Was I mistaken?"

"No. Someday I must remember to ask you what made you so confident. My name is Adah Fevre."

I nodded and thanked her.

"What did you think of the map?"

"It may be old, though clearly not as old as the paper it's drawn on." I paused. "Do you want a lecture on papers?"

Mrs. Fevre nodded, smiling. "I have nothing but time, Mr. Smithe. Time, and you. Please go ahead."

"Very well." I drew a long breath. "Modern papers are made of ponticwood fibers. Ponticwood is grown for various purposes, then sawed or split, turned on a lathe or machined by a router, drilled perhaps, sanded, and so forth. The sawdust, chips, and discarded bits used to be burned to generate steam. Now they're salvaged and pulped. Additives depend on the use to which the paper is to be put. When the proper ones have been mixed in, the pulp slurry is rolled into sheets and the sheets dried on heated rollers. Dry, they may or may not be coated; the coating (if any) depends upon the use for which the paper is intended."

"Continue, please. I'll interrupt when I have a question."

"The map paper is not that kind. It contains fibers from some fabric, probably nylon. Presumably, rags were cut up and mixed with the ponticwood stock. It would be both possible and fairly easy to make paper like that today, but there's no reason to do it. Such paper is durable, but some modern papers are even more durable. Given cool, dark, dry storage, their lives are estimated in tens of thousands of years. So why bother?"

"I understand," Mrs. Fevre said. "Please continue."

"As you wish. The map is yellowed along three edges. Only three, not four. The unyellowed edge is farthest from the spine of the book."

"I don't understand that at all."

"Yellowing results from exposure to sunlight. When a piece of paper forms a page in a book, it may yellow on three sides, the top, the bottom, and one long edge. Those three edges may see the sun. The edge bound into the spine never does."

"You think this sheet was formerly a page in a book."

"I do. Not a page of the book in which it is glued now, however; it's thicker stock, just to begin with. It would be interesting to pull it loose and see what's printed on the other side, if anything. I would not attempt that without your permission, however."

"Since the paper might tear, I withhold it. What about the map itself? Is that printed? I've wondered about it."

"No. Or at least I don't think so. It was skillfully drawn by a right-handed person, probably a man, using a pen charged with permanent ink and a straightedge—or at least it looks that way.

He was skilled and careful but not a cartographer. They normally put north at the top of their maps. That may or may not be the case here."

Mrs. Fevre asked, "No misspellings?"

"I noticed none. Did you see any?"

She shook her head, a slow, sad, gentle motion. "No, but you had a better light, and no doubt a more active mind. Mine must be flogged like a donkey until it begins to function. That map was drawn to show the reader where, and how, to find something. What does the green rectangle mean? Could it be a grave? Or a building? Something of that kind?"

I nodded. "That was my first thought, too. A grave, or perhaps a temple. A chapel, a shrine, or something of the sort. Something magical or holy."

My final remark brought a faint smile. "I take it you touched it."

That baffled me. I said, "No, I don't believe I did."

"Could there be drugs in the ink?"

"Are you saying . . . ?"

"I have touched it. Perhaps you should, too."

When I did, paper and ink slipped into my fingertips and reality slid away. I stood among a dark throng of phantom figures: a half-starved girl whose lips could not quite conceal her teeth, a leering potbellied old man, a hairy dwarf who shook three spiked balls at the end of a staff, and many more. Shadowy figures I could not see clearly and cannot quite recall.

I jerked my hand away.

"There is very little religion these days, Mr. Smithe."

Still breathless I managed, "Very little religiosity, certainly."

"Perhaps you should put down my book."

I returned it to her table. "We live in a time of peace and

prosperity." It sounded pedantic, but I pressed on. "At such times most of us feel small need to have recourse to . . ."

"You've thought of something. What is it?"

"Once when I was riding in a trailer we passed through a ruined town. A ragged child stood at the side of the road, watching us go by. Somewhere a bell tolled, just as we passed her; she turned and hurried away. I wondered about that afterward."

"Was she going to worship?" The big, dark eyes were still unreadable; the pale face held no expression.

I nodded. "That's what I concluded. With her mother, she would implore God to send them food and decent clothing. Wastepaper, sticks, or dried grass that might be burned in winter. I hope He complied."

Mrs. Fevre's voice softened. "You're not permitted money, are you? That is my understanding."

"Quite correct. No money and few personal possessions. I have this watch." I showed it to her. "We surrender our clothing in the evening and receive pajamas or nightgowns. Presumably our pockets are emptied before our clothes are washed. What is found there is seldom returned."

"It seems a miserable existence."

"We are like books. We possess the contents of our minds. A few clover leaves, like my watch, pressed between our pages. Nothing more."

"This book of mine"—Mrs. Fevre glanced at the book on her table—"possesses a map. Had you considered that?"

I smiled and shook my head. "No, I hadn't. Thank you for calling it to my attention. Does it understand what it has?"

She stared at me.

"Is the map mentioned in the text? Are there clues in the

text that might explain why the map is there? Or what that small green rectangle invokes?"

"I don't know." She shook her head. "I haven't read it, and I never thought of that."

"What drug is in the green ink? And where did you get the book?"

"It was my husband's." Mrs. Fevre sighed. "It's been years. A decade—no, more than that, Mr. Smithe. Twelve years now, I suppose. Thirteen or more."

"Do you know where he got it?"

"No." Her empty gaze was up, at the ceiling. "I have no idea."

"I don't want to pry, Mrs. Fevre; but what was his name?"

"Ah, the bookplate. Naturally you're curious. It's not his. His name was Fevre—what did I say?"

Fevre! I had missed that one and felt like kicking myself. "Never mind. I didn't intend to interrupt you."

"Dr. Barry Fevre. You've met our daughter; she must not have told you her full name."

"Correct, and I apologize for interrupting. Will you tell me a little more about your husband? It could be important."

"If you wish. The old copy asked the same thing. No doubt you'll have many of the same questions."

Well, well, I thought. Aloud I said, "Not necessarily. Was this old one from the police? A private investigator? Someone of that kind?"

"The old reclone. The library here has two of you, Mr. Smithe; I assumed you knew. Two copies, but the other one's an earlier edition. I checked him out six weeks ago and returned him, oh, eight or ten days ago. The library would never have permitted me to check you out today if I hadn't." Faintly, she smiled. "You look surprised."

"I am. I should've guessed, of course; there were several . . ." I felt as though I were choking. "Well, never mind. I haven't spoken to the old copy, Mrs. Fevre; so I may have to cover much the same ground he did. You were telling me about your husband. Barry Fevre was your husband? I believe you said so. He was Chandra's father?"

Gently, Adah Fevre nodded. "Barry and I were married, Mr. Smithe, and I was faithful. That was the name he chose for her, by the way—Chandra. She hadn't been born when he began using it. . . . I don't know where he learned the name. Does it matter?"

"Is it possible that he got it from this book?"

Mrs. Fevre shrugged. "I suppose so. As I said, I haven't read it. Or he may simply have been twitting me. My family originated in India, Mr. Smithe. We lived upon the island called Britain for four or five generations, then emigrated again. Where and why is rather a long story, and I'd prefer not to get into it."

"Then we won't. He had the book and you don't know where he got it. When did you learn of it?"

"When I cleaned out our cabin and moved here. It was in one of his bags." Mrs. Fevre paused. "Before we talk much longer you'll want a full explanation. Let me give it now; that should save some time."

My nod gave permission.

4

ADAH'S STORY

"Did you rebel against your parents, Mr. Smithe?" Adah Fevre's gentle smile softened it. "I mean hundreds and hundreds of years ago, and long before you became an author."

I smiled back. "I'm afraid so. One must, or remain a child for life. At least, that's how it seems to me when I look back; so I disobeyed and disobeyed, and eventually left them. Now I'd give everything I have or ever will have . . ."

"So did I—rebel I mean. Or at least I wanted to and quite honestly believed I had. My parents—my poor mother particularly—hoped and prayed that I would marry a doctor. I was determined not to, precisely because she did. I went out with all kinds of men, an engineer, a policeman, an athlete, a young businessman who seemed so dishonest that I felt he was sure to become rich, and so forth. The engineer bored me, the policeman married somebody else, the athlete thought much too well of himself, and the businessman was indicted and tried to borrow money from my father.

"Eventually chance led me to Barry. He and his brother

Simon taught at the university in Spice Grove. Barry was handsome, personable, intelligent, and kind; I thought of him as a professor. By the time I realized that he taught in the medical school, I was deeply in love with him. Smitten! I felt certain that I would never find a finer man. We were actually on our honeymoon before I learned that he was a doctor of medicine, an M.D." Adah Fevre laughed, a self-mocking titter. "Fate makes fools of us all, long before the end. Have you noticed?"

I admitted I had. Though I wanted to explain that I had once been married, I did not.

"Not so long ago, I was a great reader, Mr. Smithe. Now that I have unlimited time in which to read and a tablet that will make the type so large that even I can read it without my contacts, it holds no savor for me. As a child I used to read in bed when my parents thought me asleep. Stolen fruit's sweetest, you know. Tell me a story, Mr. Smithe. Will you tell me a story? Please?"

"I'd rather have you tell me a great deal more about Dr. Barry Fevre. Is this where he taught in the medical school? When you married, did you live here in Polly's Cove?"

She smiled. "No, not at all. I—I doubt that you'll understand, Mr. Smithe."

"Perhaps not. May I venture a wild guess? I expect to be wrong, but I'd like to try even so." Certain that I was right, I paused to build a little suspense. "Did you grow up in High Plains?"

"We . . . I suppose I must have told the old copy that." Adah Fevre's voice held a slight tremor. "I didn't think I had, but I suppose I must have."

"Perhaps you didn't. As I said, I haven't spoken to him. You loved Dr. Barry Fevre and married him—you just said so. What happened then?"

"We were married for three years. Barry taught and I worked in my father's business, then Barry's sabbatical year came. Do you know about those, Mr. Smithe?"

I shook my head. "Tell me."

"Tenured academics get every seventh year off—a year in which they can do anything they wish. It's a year-long paid vacation, really, although the university expects them to make good use of the time."

"I understand. Please continue."

"We had just learned that I was pregnant. The baby wouldn't come for another twenty weeks or so. Barry told me he was going to leave me while he went away to do research; he wouldn't be gone for more than six weeks at most. I could have a nice long visit with my parents—do I sound bitter, Mr. Smithe?"

"A little bitter, perhaps."

"I am. I told him he had to stay home or take me with him. I was amenable to either one of those; but if he went away leaving me alone, I would file for divorce and swear that he had deserted me. He agreed to take me with him, but he refused to tell me where we were going. He was rarely like iron, but he was then; he insisted that he didn't know the name of the place himself. It was a lie—I knew it was a lie, and he knew I knew it—but no matter what I said he stuck to it."

I found that interesting and told her so.

"Mysterious, you mean." Her voice held self-contempt. "It was. It was very mysterious, but I thought about it a lot, and eventually I got an idea. Do you want to hear it? You'll think I've gone mad, I'm sure, and it was hardly more than a—well, than intuition. A woman's intuition, and I would much prefer that we skip right over it."

I smiled. "Still, you must have confided in the old copy."

"No, Mr. Smithe, I did not. Let's forget about it. Barry explained that he was going to have to hire a boat, so we flew to the coast—"

I had raised my hand. "We've skipped over your hunch. I'd like to hear it."

Slowly, Mrs. Fevre rolled her head back and forth upon the pillow. "I'd rather not."

"You teased me with it. It may be important, and I'd like to hear it."

"All right, but please don't laugh. For some reason I felt quite sure that he was looking for cadavers."

No doubt I stared at her. "You're going to have to explain that, Mrs. Fevre."

"I shall. Barry taught anatomy, among other things. You've seen drawings of the human body. Here's where the heart is, here are the lungs, here's the stomach, and so forth. Everybody has."

I leaned forward, straining to hear.

"What the books don't tell you is that every real human body is different. The spleen may or may not be in the normal position. The small intestine may be unusually long or unusually short. You can't lick your own forehead and neither can I, but there are people who can. Doctors have to learn all that, not just where everything ought to be according to some reference, but that you can never count on its actually being there and looking the way you think it ought to look. Am I making myself clear?"

I said, "Yes. Perfectly."

"It's taught to medical students by having them dissect cadavers. This is distasteful, I know."

I agreed and urged her to go ahead with it anyway.

"Obtaining cadavers is always difficult. Some cities will allow nearby medical schools to take the corpses of derelicts—corpses that cannot be identified and do not appear to have died by violence. It would be possible, of course, to grow and sacrifice clones or even reclones, but it would be ruinously costly."

Mrs. Fevre fell silent for so long that I was afraid she would not speak again. At last she asked, "Do you know about Burke and Hare, Mr. Smithe?"

I nodded to gain a little time. "I believe I've heard of them. They pretended to be resurrection men, grave robbers who dug up fresh corpses in cemeteries and sold them to medical schools. It was a dangerous occupation, because friends and relatives of the deceased often guarded their graves. To obviate that danger, Burke and Hare murdered people in order to sell their corpses. They were caught when they killed a girl who had been flirting with some of the medical students a few hours before she turned up—still warm—on their dissection table." Talking about that centuries-old classic crime woke the memory of a bit of verse, and I managed to chant it without stumbling.

> "Through the close
> And up the stair,
> Butt an' ben wi' Burke and Hare.
> Burke's the butcher,
> Hare's the thief,
> And Knox the boy who buys the beef."

Mrs. Fevre nodded. "For years my husband had been unable to obtain as many cadavers as he needed. Very few people are willing to donate their bodies after death, although Barry and I signed the paper some years ago. People are living longer and longer, and the days when derelicts might starve in the streets are long past—there are pantries distributing surplus food and free kitchens, a great many of both. I'm told that some of the food is really quite good, and the worst of it will keep you alive." She paused, tired and discontent. "You . . . know about all that, I'm sure."

"You supposed that your husband had learned of a new source of cadavers."

"Yes, I did. And what I had guessed was precisely right. He explained that we would have to hire a boat; apparently our destination was an island off the coast or something of the sort. Hundreds of little islands, islands of small or no importance, are omitted from all but the very best maps. No doubt you know."

I shook my head. "I didn't."

"Seamen's charts used to show them. Now they get the charts on their screens, and I would think those must show them, too. I don't actually know that they do, but it seems probable since a ship might run aground there. Some of the little, unmapped islands are inhabited—one family or two, or even a dozen. Some once were but have been abandoned for years or centuries. I learned most of this from our boat, after Barry—after Barry . . ." She fell silent, visibly struggling to maintain her self-control.

"I understand." I tried to make it sympathetic.

"After he left me. Have I told you about the boat?"

"No, nothing. Tell me about it, please."

"It wasn't clean or pretty, and it certainly wasn't luxurious; but when Barry found it we had been going up and down the coast looking for something for hire that we could afford for almost two weeks. We went aboard, talked to the boat and got it to tell us how to go around and look at everything, then snapped it up. Barry paid its price, as he told me afterward. He had been so afraid of losing it that he just authorized a draft for the full amount the boat had asked."

I said, "I understand. Tell me a little about this boat, please. Describe it as well as you can. I know you're not a sailor; I'm not either."

"All right. It was a fishing boat, not just a sailboat. There are laws about how long the boats can fish. Do you know about those?"

I shook my head.

"Each year they're limited to so many days. If they can catch a lot in that time, all right. If they catch next to nothing, that's their bad luck. Every year all the boats go out on the first fishing day. They fish day and night, no rest for the crew and no maintenance for the boat. I can't imagine what they're like on the last day, practically wrecked, I suppose. There are refrigerated bins down under the main deck; if a boat's been lucky, those bins are full or nearly full of fish and the boat receives lots of money, enough to pay its crew, maintain itself, and pass a good profit up to its owners. If it hasn't been lucky at all, the boat and its crew have worked like slaves for next to nothing. It must be a terribly hard existence."

Completely unable to guess where this was going, I agreed.

"Most fishing boats just stay in port when the fishing days are over, but this one remained as active as it could, trying to make a little extra money here and there. If two or three people wanted to go out to one of the islands, it would take them. Whenever they were ready to come back, or whenever some island people wanted to visit the mainland, it would go out and pick them up. It took sportsmen deep-sea fishing for so much a day." Adah Fevre paused.

When I did not speak, she said, "Sport fishing is still allowed if you have a license. It has to be hook-and-line, though." She paused again, sighing audibly. "Electrodes and nets are not permitted."

"Your husband chartered this boat," I said. "Do you know the terms of the agreement?"

"Only what it told me. It was to follow the course that Barry had laid down, and tell Barry immediately about anything it saw. It was to wake up Barry if he were asleep."

"Any land?"

"Yes. Or any other boats, or ships, or things floating in the water. Birds flying over. Anything at all."

The list puzzled me, but I tried not to let it show. I asked, "Where did your husband get off the boat?"

"I don't know. First, I think I ought to tell you about the cabins." Mrs. Fevre hesitated, her head still on the pillow, her big dark eyes staring blindly up at the ceiling and never sparing a glance for me. "There were three, a large, comfortable cabin and two smaller cabins. It charged more for the big cabin, of course."

I said, "Go on, please."

"That one had two bunks, one above the other, a table, four chairs, a stove, and so forth. Two closets, too."

"I take it that when you and your husband were on board

there were no other fully humans, no clones, and no 'bots. No other passengers of any kind. Correct?"

Her nod was almost imperceptible. "That's how it was. We bought two new mattresses and sheets and blankets for our bunks before we put out. The boat didn't mind. It was glad to get them, Barry told me."

"I'm sure it was."

"We had brought a good deal of luggage. I, at least, didn't know where we were going or how long we'd be gone. I brought some summer things and some warm things. A lot of cosmetics, too; soap and several towels, plus some odds and ends I thought Barry might need. I had five bags." She paused. "A set of matched luggage."

I nodded.

"Barry was almost as bad, three large bags. One was too heavy for me to lift. I remember that, because I had to hire a longshoreman to carry our luggage ashore for me when we came back to port."

I said, "This was after your husband disappeared, I assume."

"Yes. I went back to the hotel—"

"Tell me about Barry's disappearance, please. I'm afraid we've skipped over that."

"There's next to nothing to tell. We sailed slowly at night. I was told that there's always a danger of ramming something. We had a searchlight and radar, but even so . . . a big light isn't the same as daylight, after all."

"Didn't your boat sleep at night?"

Mrs. Fevre shook her head. "No, never, at least as far as I know. The boat was driving itself all night, just like a ground-car."

"I see. Go on."

"One night I woke up and the boat was shaking Barry's bunk. I was in the lower bunk, and Barry in the upper bunk. Perhaps I told you about that?"

I waved it away.

"It was shaking his bunk and telling Barry something. I don't know what—I was half-asleep. Barry got up, climbing down past my bunk, and went out on deck in his pajamas." She sighed. "It's painful to say this, but I went back to sleep. All this had happened before, you understand, over and over. Sometimes twice or three times in one night."

She fell silent until I said, "Please continue."

"When I got up, Barry had gone. I thought he was out on deck, so I got dressed and went outside; we usually ate breakfast together. He wasn't there. It was so foggy I couldn't be sure, so I went wandering around the deck in the fog, calling for him. Eventually the boat got my attention and told me he had left. Another boat had come hours before I left our cabin, and Barry had gone aboard."

As though she feared that I hadn't been listening, she added, "Our boat said Barry had gotten into this other boat and sailed away. That was all I could get out of it."

"What did you do?"

"I told the boat I wanted to keep going, I wanted it to follow Barry's instructions. It wouldn't listen to that. It said that Barry had given new instructions, telling it to return to Polly's Cove, and that was what it was doing. Barry had paid it. Barry alone had signed its charter. I—well I tried half a dozen arguments. I'd prefer not tell you what they were."

When I did not speak Adah added, "None of them worked."

I nodded. "Then don't tell me."

"We went back. The boat wanted the rest of its money, the entire amount, but I didn't think it deserved it. Its owners got in touch with me and threatened to sue me for it, but—"

"Before all that, didn't you question your boat about the one that had taken your husband away?"

"Oh, yes. I don't believe it knew a lot, and it had trouble expressing what little it knew. It said the other boat had been a lugger." Adah Fevre paused. "That's just another kind of sailboat, as I understand it. There had been several people on it, men and women. It had come close to us and had told our boat to heave to—reverse the engine so as to stop and so on. Barry had gone to the rail and talked to the people on board. After a minute or two he had gone over the side and into the boat . . . into this lugger. Then they pushed off and sailed away with him. I asked whether Barry had taken a bag, and the boat said it didn't think so; but one of Barry's bags was gone."

"Just one?"

She nodded. "There was a big fight with the owners when I got back here. I didn't want to pay them anything, and they were going to sue. I talked to their lawyer, and we agreed on a certain amount for each day we had been at sea. I paid that—it wasn't as much as the full fee—and that settled it."

"Do you know the name of the boat?"

Mrs. Fevre tried to remember it for so long that I almost interrupted her with another question. At last she said, "The *Third Sister*. That was it—or anyway I think it was."

I said, "Please tell me about finding this book. The map was already glued in back when you found it?"

"Yes. Yes, it was. There's a little hotel here. It's not even a chain hotel, an independent I suppose you'd call it, the Polly's Cove Inn. Barry and I had stayed there until Barry found the boat—it had a name, something about women. I've been trying to think of it."

"The *Third Sister*? That's what you said."

"I—I don't think so, Mr. Smith. Your name is Smith, isn't it? Like that other one?"

"Yes, with a final E. I take it you went back to the Polly's Cove Inn after you left the boat?"

"I did. I stayed there for a week, I think. I kept thinking that I ought to go back to High Plains alone and—and explain about Barry; but I kept hoping he'd come back. Another day. Just one more day . . . How long has it been now? Year and years. I'm afraid I've lost track of time, but I'm still waiting."

"Where were you living when Chandra was born?"

"Here. Not in the Inn. Here, in this house. I remember bringing her home. I was thinking—I kept thinking over and over that there was no one I could show her to, but I was wrong. Mrs. Heuse was waiting for us. Standing there in the doorway, waiting for us. I showed her Chandra, and I was so proud. So proud and happy! I thought—I still tried to believe that Barry would come back any day, and then I would show her to him. Tell him he had a daughter. Only . . ." Adah sighed.

"Yes?"

"He never came back. He will, though. I'm quite certain of that, Mr. Smithe. He'll come back when he can. Just as soon as he can."

I said, "You must have left the Polly's Cove Inn and bought this house."

Mrs. Fevre's head moved slowly from side to side. "I rented

it. I rent it still—it's very cheap. I have an eephone, and Chandra calls the people for me. I authorize a withdrawal. I sold our house in High Plains. I had to, and it brought a great deal of money. . . . Homes are so costly there."

"Because of the university, I suppose."

"We had a very nice house. It wasn't as large as this one, though. This one has a great many rooms; I've never counted them. They're empty. Most of the rooms are almost empty. This is my furniture. I bought it. . . . I'm sure I bought it. Nearly certain . . ."

I said, "I'm tiring you, I know. You must have opened your husband's bags, the two he had left on the boat. Was this book in one of them?"

"Yes. The *Third Sister*. That was the name of our boat. The *Third Sister*."

I asked another question but received no reply. Adah Fevre was asleep.

5

A Cold Tea Party

Chandra was waiting in the hall when I opened the door. I cleared my throat and told her, "I see you were listening. I thought you might be." If it sounded grown-up and not at all friendly, well, I tried.

She nodded silently and would not meet my eyes. There wasn't the ghost of a grin.

"I'm going to the kitchen now, and you might as well come along." She was a good kid, so I tried to make it kind, adding, "That will be more dignified, and I'll be glad to have you along."

We found Mrs. Heuse sitting on a three-legged stool at the little kitchen table and looking thoughtful. I knew, or at least I thought I knew, as soon as I got a good look at her face; when I had gotten settled in the rickety old ponticwood chair across the table from her and had a chance to study her face, I knew for certain: she was a reclone, like me. Some people say there are tiny facial flaws that get fixed before birth for fully human kids but not for us; still, people seldom notice ours consciously. Maybe that's the truth, but whether it's true or not I don't consciously notice the flaws most of the time. In case you ever need to know for certain and can't find any flaws, here's a sure-fire test: if the left side of the face mirrors the right side perfectly, that's a fully human. Guaranteed.

Trying to make it friendly, I said, "I imagine you're mulling over what to make for lunch."

Looking up, she shook her head. "No, sir. Are you a guest here? A guest of Mrs. Fevre's? Lunch is already in the steamer, but if you have special needs I'll be happy to see what I can do."

I shook my head. "I'm a reclone, Mrs. Heuse. Mrs. Fevre sent Chandra to borrow me from the Polly's Cove Public Library. I have no special requirements, and you wouldn't be obliged to satisfy them if I did. Do you by any chance know Millie Baumgartner? The woman who wrote so many cookbooks? I'm a friend of hers."

Chandra stepped in. "He's all right, Mrs. Heuse. I'm pretty sure we can trust him."

"I know about Millicent Baumgartner's books. . . ." Mrs. Heuse hesitated, wanting to call me *sir* but knowing I was no better than an equal. "I have two of them, and from time to time Chandra brings me others from the library. Her book on pastries is really wonderful, the best I've ever seen."

"There's a copy of Millie herself in the library now. Not permanently, but on interlibrary loan. I thought you might have requested her."

Mrs. Heuse shook her head, and Chandra said, "I didn't, either."

I said, "Technically, she's a reclone. A moment ago I told you I'm one. You are aware of that, I'm sure."

The answer came slowly. "Yes. I surely am."

"Chandra would have called for you, presumably, saying that her mother wanted you. She could pick Millie up in the same way, I imagine."

Chandra nodded.

"Do I have to say it?" Once again, *sir* almost popped out.

I wanted to sigh. "I see. You're overdue, and afraid I'll blow the whistle. I won't. Not now, and not if I ever get back to my shelf."

Chandra said, "She's been here for almost two years. Mother told me to say we'd lost her, so I did. Then Mother had to pay up—surrender her deposit is what they call it. So she did. So now Mrs. Heuse belongs to us. We like it that way, and so does she."

"They'll never burn me here," Mrs. Heuse told me. "Mrs. Fevre has promised me that, and she's a good woman. She'll keep her promise."

Of course I agreed, even though I felt a whole lot less certain than I sounded. Certainty and sincerity can be awfully hard to fake, but now and then I manage.

"They'll reclaim me if they find me in the library, sir." (She had given up the fight.) "You must know what kind of people they are down there."

I admitted I didn't, and tried to explain that I was on interlibrary loan and had only just arrived.

"They will. That Ms. Prentice would brand me noncirculating and give back Mrs. Fevre's money, and there would be nothing Mrs. Fevre could do short of suing."

"Which she wouldn't undertake." I nodded. "I get it. Mrs. Heuse, I'm looking into several matters at Mrs. Fevre's request."

"I know that, sir."

"You can help me with one of them easily and quickly, and I feel quite certain that you will. When the lights go out, something black gets into Mrs. Fevre's bedchamber—how, I don't know. It flattens itself on the floor and crawls toward Mrs. Fevre, crying—or at least Chandra calls it crying. Since she's heard it, I believe at least twice, I think it wise to trust her terminology. Whimpering, whining, and sobbing, I believe. Speaking a few short words. I know you know more about it than she and I do, and I want you to tell us now. Tell us, and I'll guarantee that you won't be punished for whatever you may have done."

Mrs. Heuse stared, her lower lip trembling. Chandra hugged her and tried to comfort her, motioning urgently for me to leave.

I nodded and said, "Explain that I'm not going to harm your mother's dog." Soon after that, I walked back to the library alone.

Lunch was over by the time I got there, and it would be hours before dinner. When I'd finished looking at maps on one of the screens, I stood up, rubbed my eyes, and thought things over. I was hungry, but then I was always hungry, just as somebody had told me once. I knew that reading cookbooks would make me even hungrier, but duty is duty; so I trudged off to page through a dozen, mostly on a screen but a few on yellowing paper.

Elizabeth Heuse had written *One Hour Company Dinners*, *Luncheon for Two in Fifteen Minutes*, and *Fifty-four Truly Delicious Snacks Your Family Has Never Tasted*. I was just starting on a chapter of that last one when Millie caught up with me.

"Don't tell me you're taking up cooking, Ern!" She made it mock-serious.

"Nope," I told her, "I've taken up starving. Some of this stuff looks wonderful."

"Quite a few of them really are if you can find the ingredients. That book has a habit of calling for cheeses most nutrition services have never heard of."

"I see. What was she like in person, Millie? You must have known her."

"Not very well." Millie paused thoughtfully. "Are you going to tell me why you want to find out about her?"

I shook my head. "Please don't try to guess."

"I already have, but I won't fuss and stamp to make you tell me whether I'm right. She seemed withdrawn and a little bit sad when I knew her. Have you noticed how rarely she mentions beef and chicken?"

I shook my head again.

"Eating fish doesn't seem to trouble her, but birds and animals? Those did, both of them."

"Birds and mammals."

Millie's shoulders rose and fell. "I stand corrected. She was an animal lover. I was in the audience one time when some man asked her how to roast a dog. He was trying to be funny, but she froze. Absolutely froze. Finally the woman who'd introduced her stepped in and told the man how to grill a hot dog. After that somebody else announced a ten-minute break. The stage went dark and just about all the audience filed out, I think mostly to the restrooms. Fifteen or twenty minutes later, when almost everybody had come back, Betty Heuse was in control of herself again. Do you want to hear more about that?"

I nodded.

"You never sit down, do you?"

We went over to a table, where I held her chair until she sat. I took the one next to hers.

"You do know how to operate these four-legged chair things. I was beginning to wonder."

"I wonder about a lot of things," I told her. "Particularly my patron."

"You haven't been returned?"

"No. I came back hoping for lunch, but I was too late."

"Your patron wasn't going to feed you?"

I shook my head. "She was asleep. Her cook was going to feed us—that's my patron's daughter and me—but I had upset her and the near future didn't look good. I came back to have a look at dog books and cookbooks, but I haven't gotten anywhere with the dog books yet."

"You've had an interesting time of it, Ern. I'm no detective, but I know the signs."

"Yes, I have. Very."

Millie glanced around before speaking again. "Talking it over with me might help."

"All right, here goes. Do you know a lot about dogs?"

Silently, she shook her head.

"Neither do I." I stopped to think, sort of hoping that Millie would go away. "Once I told a lady I knew more about dogs than I do about kids, and that's not exactly a lie."

"But you still don't know much."

"Correct, because my knowledge is out of date. I looked through a couple of dog books before I started on the cookbooks. They told me that there are at least two dozen breeds I've never heard of, and which breeds are the best talkers; but they didn't tell me the kind of thing I need to find out."

"What is it your patron wants you to find out? Maybe I can help."

I took a good, deep breath and let go of it in a sigh. "What she really wants is a detective, but why pay a lot of money for one when you can borrow a reclone resource from the library for nothing?"

"You're saying that fully human detectives are expensive?"

I nodded. "The good ones are. Very."

"She may not have the money. Besides, I doubt that there are any detectives we could hire here. This is just a village, Ern."

"I know. A private investigator might be as ignorant of Polly's Cove—and the sea—as I am. But the author of Sherlock Holmes might really help, and so might the guys who wrote Ellery Queen, or even the one who wrote about Long John Silver and Jim. . . ."

"You've hit on something. What is it?"

"Jim Hawkins." I took a good deep breath. "Do you know that book?"

"*Treasure Island?* Yes, I do. My father read it to us, and I read it to my grandchildren. It seemed terribly dated to me, but that didn't bother my grandchildren." Millie was getting out a handkerchief.

"This was in your first life, of course."

"Y-y-yes. Way, way back. I've looked in the screens, Ern, t-trying to find out what became of those children; what their lives had been like and how they died. I'd love to know. This can't possibly interest you."

It did, and I told her so.

"I remember their names, of course, and the names of their mothers and fathers; but I could never be certain. . . ."

"I understand."

Millie's sigh was almost a moan. "Let's talk about something else. What does your patron want?"

"It's complicated. One complication is that I feel I really have two. Legally, Mrs. Fevre checked me out. Her name's on the record, and she put up the deposit. But her daughter—"

Millie laid a gentle hand on my arm. "In that case Mrs. Fevre's your patron, Ern. You know that."

"I agree. She was the one who asked the library to borrow me from Spice Grove as well, but she didn't come to the library to pick me up and take me home. Her daughter Chandra did that. Because she did, I can't help but feel that Chandra's morally my patron. Or that she's my patron too; take your choice." I shut up for a minute, not wanting to add what I knew I had to say. "Chandra's still a kid."

Millie chuckled softly. "You'd never betray a patron, and you're too soft-hearted to disappoint a child. No wonder I like you."

"All right, if that's the way you want it. Yes. The patrons have different problems. Those problems may or may not be interrelated; it's much too soon to tell." I stopped talking to sweep aside lovely pictures of dogs all bathed and brushed, and food so neat and perfect that I would have been ashamed to eat it.

"What's the little girl's?"

"A dark—she thinks black—creature that gets into her mother's bedroom at night and crawls toward her mother crying. By *crying* she means whining and whimpering, or so I think. Sometimes it talks a little."

"Interesting!"

"Yes, isn't it. She and her mother yell at it and tell it to go away, at which it seems to disappear."

"This is at night? Any lights in the room?"

"None were mentioned."

"Then disappearing should be easy."

"I'm afraid so. But when Chandra searches the room, there's no sign of it."

"But you think it's a dog."

I nodded. "I think it behaves like one, except for the disappearing."

Millie considered. "What does this have to do with Long John Silver?"

"The mother's problem is quite different. She has a map. It looks like a treasure map, and it may be one, but it never actually says that's what it is. Apparently it belonged to her missing husband."

"Well, well, well! And where is Treasure Island?"

I shook my head. "We don't know, Millie. The map doesn't say."

"It doesn't say, but Mrs. Fevre thinks you know how to find out. She must, or she wouldn't have borrowed you."

"There may be other reasons, or at least that's how it seems to me. I hadn't thought of enlisting your help, but now that I have—" I stood up. "Let's go to the lobby."

"Prentice and some other woman are on the desk, both of them busy."

"Good. We'll hope that it keeps up."

When we had ducked and weaved through the crowd, we found that the bench on which the older copy of me had sat was empty. "Did you see him?" I asked Millie. "You knew about Prentice and the other librarian. Did you see the earlier copy of me sitting here?"

She shook her head.

"An old man with one arm. He was me in another forty years, a much earlier edition for sale and quite cheaply."

"You're saying this library has had another copy of you for years and years."

"Not quite, but it's very probable."

"Then why would they borrow you from Spice Grove?"

"An old, damaged copy," I said. Someone bumped me and apologized. I said, "I could speculate, but let's find him and ask."

Somebody else bumped me and just about knocked me down. My left foot slipped, and I grabbed Millie to keep from falling.

"Here now!" She steadied me. "Lucky for you I'm so solid."

I thanked her. "Let's get out—"

"What is it, Ern?"

There was blood on my left shoe.

Shaking my head, I sat down on the bench; a few seconds later, Millie sat beside me. Maybe she said something then. If she did, I have forgotten it.

Gradually, the crowd thinned out. A dozen people, then eight or ten, then three or four. It was quite a bit later than I had expected, but at last Prentice left.

I nudged Millie. "I already owe you a bunch of favors, I know that. Will you do something more for me?"

"Yes, if you'll tell me what's up."

"This isn't the time for it. Go over there across the room, and go up to that librarian. I want you on that patron's left. Try to slip in a question, something that can't be answered with a yes or no. If she tries to shoo you away stay right there. If she answers your question, ask her another—anything you like, but nothing about me. Will you do that?"

"All right, but you'll owe me. A lot."

I waited until the librarian had turned toward Millie before I pulled the lifeless body of the earlier copy of Ern A. Smithe from behind the bench. Several patrons stared, and a woman gasped. I ignored them.

When I picked up the bloodstained sign that had announced the price of the dead me and put it around what was left of his neck, one of the men laughed. Patting down this late Ern A. Smithe's pockets yielded a key on a cheap violet key ring that might have been the prize in some sort of children's game. Muttering a promise I knew the other copy of me could not hear, I dropped it into my pocket.

Across the lobby, I touched Millie's elbow. "Come on, you can bother this librarian some other time." She nodded, and followed me to a table where I held her chair as before.

When we were both seated, she whispered, "What was all that about, Ern? I enjoyed it, but what were you doing? Tell me the truth."

"I took an old reclone from under that bench and set him up on it again. He was dead." The horror of the thing filled my mind; I shook my head to clear it. "Somebody had cut his throat."

Millie stared.

"A small blade, or anyway I think it was. Small and very sharp." That had been easy, but the next part hurt. "I'm afraid he may have done it himself."

"Did he belong to this library?" She was trying to change the subject.

"I believe so, although they may have gotten him the same way they got us. Mrs. Fevre had checked him out earlier. He seems to have investigated for her, and I was looking forward to talking with him. Somebody else got to him first. I don't know what they said or did, but it made him take his own life."

"What did he write? What was his name?"

"Mysteries. His byline was Ern A. Smithe. That's 'Smith,' with a silent 'E' on the end."

It hung in the air between us while Millie's mouth formed a neat pink O. At last she said, "He was you, so you must have found out something."

"Or someone thought he had, or feared he might. I agree."

"Wasn't he here in the lobby before we came out here? You said something about that."

"Correct. He was."

"Then somebody may have seen something."

"I agree with that too. The question is, who was it? Who did? Assuming he or she exists." Two 'bots had come in. One was wheeling a big trash bin, and the other had two mops and a bucket. We got up and watched from the doorway while they put Ern A. Smithe's body into the trash bin and began to mop up his blood. Pretty soon one extended an arm to pick up what looked like a ruler-sized piece of shiny, silvery metal. For a few seconds he held it in front of his eyes before dropping it into his trash bin.

Millie whispered, "Aren't they destroying evidence?"

"Perhaps, but I searched his pockets a moment ago, and we couldn't stop them; they have their orders. Prentice must have seen him before she left. Possibly someone told her afterward. She will have ordered the 'bots to collect the body, burn it, and mop the floor."

"It should be a crime. We ought to be able to call the police, have them investigate. All that."

I smiled. "Bring the killer to justice."

"Exactly."

"We should be able to; but as things stand, it isn't murder, just destruction of property. He belonged to this library, presumably. If someone else killed him, they can be forced to pay the price the library was asking for him. . . ." I pursed my lips.

"What is it?"

"Chandra! The little girl. That's what he's come for—Chandra." I was on my feet again, although I could not remember standing.

A new voice: "Aaah, there you are, Mrs. Baumgartner."

It was another 'bot.

"You're being checked out, and your patron has come for you. Come along."

Millie sighed, shrugged, and followed the 'bot out. I tagged along behind.

The patron had collected Rose already and was waiting for Millie in the lobby, taller than I had expected and quite a bit younger in appearance. He looked older than Rose but much younger than Millie.

Had I been wrong about Chandra?

When I saw they were getting into a hovercab, I went back inside and waited for a chance to quiz the librarian at the desk. "Wasn't that Dr. Fevre?"

"Yes, it was. Have you met him?"

I shook my head. "I've been at their house, though. Mrs. Fevre has me checked out now."

"Really? You've come back here with her permission, I hope."

I nodded and smiled. "Of course. I've been looking into diets and dogs for her. I've never met her husband, but I saw his picture there. I don't suppose you know what he wants with Millie Baumgartner?"

"Her culinary skills, I imagine."

I agreed, and said I ought to be getting back to Mrs. Fevre's.

Outside, Millie, Rose, and the doctor were already gone. I strolled down the hill and hiked up the next to the high white house with the widow's walk. They weren't there, either.

Chandra was eating a sandwich in the kitchen. "Would you like one of these, Mr. Smithe? Mrs. Heuse will fix you one if I ask her to."

"Or if you tell me you want one," Mrs. Heuse said. Her nose and eyes were red, but she had dried her tears. "We're friends, I hope."

I tried to smile back. "Very good friends, even if you think I ought to make my own sandwiches."

"That won't be necessary, sir." She was getting bread out of the freezer. "White, sourdough, or rye? There's probably some whole wheat around here somewhere, if you'd like that."

I cleared my throat. "Any of the three. Your choice."

Softly, Chandra asked what was bothering me.

"Later." I wasn't sure I knew myself. "When we're alone."

That got me a nod and a quick smile. "How about if we eat out on the patio? I can show you the garden."

"I'd love to see it."

Mrs. Heuse brought me my sandwich and a big mug of steaming tea, and Chandra and I carried our food down a short hall I had not seen before.

There was a toolshed and an old greenhouse that was clearly no longer in use. Other than those, half a dozen flowerbeds that in summer appeared to have held lilies or day lilies, irises and roses. Better than any of these, a small paved patio with a round tile-topped table, a big yellow umbrella, and four low-backed chairs. Chandra opened the umbrella and positioned it to block the wind while I set down my plate, napkin, and mug and made myself at home.

When she had finished and seated herself in front of her half-eaten sandwich and mug of cocoa, I said, "I told one of the librarians a lie this afternoon."

"Really? No kidding?" She grinned at me. "I bet it was the very first time in your whole life."

I shook my head. "It wasn't, but I think it may have been the first time here in Polly's Cove. I told her that I had seen a picture of your father—Dr. Fevre's your father, isn't he?"

"As far as I know."

"'It's a wise child who knows her own father.' You know about all that, I see. I told the librarian I'd seen a picture of Dr. Fevre here in this house. That was the lie. I have not, not even one. Want to tell me why?"

"Mother hid them." After that Chandra was quiet, waiting for another question. When I said nothing, she added, "They made her cry. Everything would be like regular, then she'd look at his picture—there used to be one in her room, it was a picture of them standing together—and a close-up of him in front of the house. She made that one talk to her sometimes, but two or three years ago she took them both down."

"Do you know where they are?"

"Sure. In the closet in his room, up on the shelf. I haven't looked at them for a long time now, but that's where they used to be. Why'd you tell that librarian you'd seen his picture?"

"Because it's one of the best ways to find out who someone you don't know is. If you simply ask, the person you're talking to says, 'Why do you want to know?' They say that half the time, anyway. Probably more. But if you say, 'Wasn't that Jake Gibson, the oldest Gibson boy?' they may say, 'No, that's Phil Robinson.'"

Chandra stared for a moment. "I see. . . ."

"Besides, I had a hunch. There aren't a lot of reclone resources in Polly's Cove, but three of us have been loaned to the Polly's Cove Public Library, all three of us from the Spice Grove Public Library. That was quite a coincidence, if it was a coincidence."

She nodded slowly.

"You've got to put up a hefty deposit to check out a reclone. How many people here have that kind of money?"

"I don't know."

"Then guess. Half a dozen? More?"

"No way." Chandra shook her head. "Two or three people, maybe, besides my mother."

"You're probably right. I'd certainly think there are fewer than ten. Even nine would be surprising. Your mother had requested me. She'd consulted an older, damaged copy. Eventually she had given up on him, or somehow been forced to return him. Then she'd requested a newer copy. There aren't a lot of us."

"Sorry to hear that." Chandra actually sounded sorry. "I bet you'd like to be more popular."

"To confess the truth, I don't care much. I wanted to sell better during my first life because I needed the money. Today, I just want to be checked out often, because they won't burn me as long as I am. But if every library on this continent had a copy of me, I myself, this copy"—I tapped my chest—"would be checked out somewhat less, not more. Do you think you'd recognize your father if he sat down at our table now?"

"Probably." Chandra paused. "From the pictures, mostly. I really don't remember him all that well."

"Seven years? I think that's what your mother said. Were you on the boat with them?"

She shook her head.

"You can't have been here. Your mother didn't rent this house until she came back; so where were you?"

"At Aunt Laura's house in High Plains. I kind of remember it a little. Not much."

"Naturally. Let's get back to the original question. Why were three of us—that's Millie Baumgartner, Rose Romain, and me—all borrowed from the same library at the same time? I think I may know the answer, although I could be wrong."

Chandra put down her sandwich. "And you're going to tell me, right? Because it has something to do with me?"

"Yes, but it's mostly just to clear my head. Your mother thinks your father has gone to some mysterious island. The map she showed me is supposed to be of that island." When Chandra said nothing, I added, "You probably know about her map."

"Sure. You don't think it's real?"

"No. I think it's probably a red herring—a false clue created by someone who wanted to throw your mother, and anyone she might find to help her, off the track. There are a number of small islands northeast of this continent, Cape Breton, Prince Edward, and a good scattering of others smaller still." I smiled. "I've been looking at maps on one of the library screens. No doubt it shows."

"Sure you have. Nobody'd know about that unless they looked it up."

"Go along the ragged coast of Greenland, and there are still more. East of Greenland you'll find the island called Iceland, which our ancestors considered the end of the world. It's right on the Arctic Circle; and if this world needs an end, that's as good a place as any."

"All these islands must be awfully cold."

"They are, cold and rocky." I smiled, trying to keep it light. "If you're looking for a tropical paradise, you're headed in the wrong direction."

"You don't think that island my father's supposed to be on is real. Am I right?"

"You are. Let's forget for a minute or two about your parents' voyage and the lugger. Put those aside. Where has your father been, and what has he been doing? What do you think?"

Chandra considered. "He can't have been around here, or anyway not much."

"Because your mother would see him?"

"Most likely, she wouldn't. She doesn't go out a lot."

"Because you'd see him, in that case."

"Well, maybe. Only I'm not really sure I'd know him from the pictures if he didn't stop to talk or something." Chandra paused, thinking. "This is an awfully small town."

"He could have grown a beard, couldn't he? Changed his name? Maybe had plastic surgery?"

"You're putting me on, Mr. Smithe. That's not nice."

"Only a little bit. I saw him in the library, as I told you. He didn't have a beard then. Does he have one in those pictures we ought to look at?"

Chandra shook her head.

"I didn't think so. I'd think that plastic surgery wouldn't be much use unless he changed his name as well. You'll agree, I hope?"

"Sure."

"When I asked the librarian whether the man I'd seen was Dr. Fevre, she agreed at once that it was. Clearly she knew him as Dr. Fevre. As for where he was—how long has it been since you've spoken to your Aunt Laura?"

Chandra looked baffled. "Forever. She never visits or anything."

"Is she your mother's sister? Do you know?"

"Sure I know—I know all about that. She's my father's kid sister."

I thought that over. "Do you have a screen in your room?"

"You bet I do. You just about have to have one for school."

"Fine," I said. "We can use that. Since we know your Aunt Laura's first and last names and where she lives, we shouldn't have a lot of trouble finding her; but if we do, there's the university. We can check with them."

"You think he's there?"

I nodded. "It's very probable. From what I've been told, he's a tenured professor. People with tenure rarely move around—or resign, either. Every fully human needs some source of income. We reclones have none, which makes us much more conscious of that than we ought to be."

"Don't you get your food at the library?"

"Certainly. We eat whatever the librarians choose to feed us, which has to be enough to keep us looking like the pictures taken during our first lives. We sleep on our shelves, and we're issued clean clothing every morning. I bought us two steaming creamys, remember?"

"Sure."

"I'm an adult and you're still a child—"

"I'm almost thirteen!"

"Meaning that you won't be considered fully grown for another five years. I was going to say that most reclones couldn't have done that, because they wouldn't have enough money." I was skirting a lie here; the reason should be obvious.

"I could give you a little if you want me to."

I could not help smiling. "You're very kind. I won't ask for it unless I need it."

"All right." Chandra took a bite of her sandwich and chewed it thoughtfully. When she had swallowed, she said, "Suppose my father is back in High Plains, like you think. What are we going to do then?"

I sighed. "First, let me say that I don't think he's there now. Shall I explain why?"

She nodded.

"First, because I just saw him in the library here picking up Millie Baumgartner and Rose Romain. If he has returned to High Plains already he must have a flitter, which I think is actually quite possible. Furthermore, he must have taken them there with him, which I think extremely improbable."

Stubbornly, "He could do that if he wanted to."

"No doubt he could. Still, I doubt very much that he did. Just look at it. They were in the Spice Grove Public Library with me. He requested that the library here get them on interlibrary loan just as it was getting me. Why do that if he intended to return them to Spice Grove as soon as he had them?"

Chandra thought that one over. At last she said, "It would have to be because he wanted to show them to somebody here."

"I would reverse that. I'm quite sure that there's someone in Spice Grove whom he wants to prevent from seeing them—certainly from seeing them with him."

"And if they're here, that person in Spice Grove couldn't see them at all."

"Correct, save for the pictures on the covers of their books."

Chandra finished her cocoa. "I still don't understand why all three had to come from the same place. Have you figured that out, too?"

"I don't think it was necessary, just that it was probable. As I understand it, a professor is not granted a sabbatical until he has gotten tenure. Getting tenure generally takes ten years or more. That means your father probably taught in Spice Grove for at least ten years before he came here with your mother. Libraries don't buy writers like me—or like Millie or Rose, for that matter—unless there is a good deal of interest at their libraries in those writers. Reclones are costly, but if they are checked out a lot, there will be no problem with the Board."

Chandra nodded.

"When I spoke to your mother, she told me that she used to be a great reader. Since she asked the library for the help of a mystery writer, myself, she has presumably read a great many mysteries. She may have read some books of other kinds as well, but she almost certainly read a round dozen mysteries every year. Quite possibly more."

"She talks about them sometimes."

"I imagine so. We all talk, at least occasionally, about the things we read. No doubt she bought a few mysteries to read, and she may well have been given some; but it's almost certain that a great many came from the Mystery section in the Polly's

Cove Public Library. Millie told me once that they had more of her books in Cooking than all the other authors combined."

"You think my father's learning to cook." Chandra sounded dubious.

I shook my head. "I think he learned about Mrs. Heuse. Are there any other servants in this household?"

"Only Mrs. Snow. She's the housekeeper."

"Then he may have learned about it from her, or from Mrs. Heuse herself, or from one of the librarians. Now, when he wants a good cook who will be powerless to resign, he has decided to do the same thing." I shrugged. "It's even possible that he learned about someone whose name we have never heard doing what he wanted to do. If he did, he may have mentioned it to your mother one day over kafe, unintentionally planting the idea."

Slowly Chandra said, "I see. . . ."

"Or he may have thought of it for himself."

6

From Library Custody

Aunt Laura turned out to be a whole lot harder than I had expected. She was not at home—or if she was, she wasn't answering her screen. Tenaciously questioned by Chandra, the Spice Grove Public Library supplied the title of the *Greater Spice Grove Area Almanac Atlas & Directory*, a surprisingly useful reference "book" that (deep sigh!) did not actually exist on paper.

"Books," I told Chandra, "ought to exist. They ought to be actual physical objects you can pick up and put down. We should not have to engage a medium and hold a séance."

She gave me a you-sure-are-weird look.

"You don't see why."

"No, I don't!" (Spoken with heavy emphasis on the final word.) "It would take a ton of paper."

"You're absolutely right. Still, it might mean that only books worth reading would achieve wide circulation."

"If you say so."

She sounded dubious; and now that I've had time to think about it, I know she was right.

A screen search of this phantom Area Almanac gave us Laura Fevre's address, and much later and only grudgingly the names and addresses of several residents of apartments and houses in the area. The screens Chandra made to a dozen of them got us only negative information. Not one of Aunt Laura's neighbors knew where she had gone or whether she might return to her home later today. One helpful lady suggested half a dozen probable destinations however, and another, about twenty minutes later, gave us Aunt Laura's eephone number, a detail none of her other neighbors had admitted to knowing. This time I screened, feeling that I would have to fine-tune my later questions to Aunt Laura Fevre's first replies. After a deep breath and a brave smile I began my call by politely hoping that I was not interfering with her shopping.

"Oh, I'm not shopping, Mr. Smithe. I'm at work." Aunt Laura looked and sounded younger than I had expected. "What can I do for you?"

"First let me explain that I'm trying to help out your brother's wife, Adah Fevre. I'm sure you know that your brother is married; I'm told that you took care of little Chandra for your brother and his wife some years ago."

"I did. Barry and his wife are separated, though; and his wife has custody of their daughter. Is this something about Chandra?"

"Only indirectly. It's urgent that Adah get in touch with Barry, however. Do you know where he is?"

"Yes, he's on sabbatical."

I nodded. Seven years since they had chartered the *Three Sisters*; I ought to have thought of that. "Where he is physically. Chandra and I need to talk to him."

"Really, I have no idea." Aunt Laura paused, looking thoughtful. "Couldn't he be off where he gets all those cadavers for his classes? I know he goes there and comes back with cadavers. I believe it's some island or other."

I took a deep breath. "I suppose he could. Do you know where it is?"

"Why, I haven't the foggiest idea. It sounds like a perfectly awful place, though. Have you talked to Peggy?"

I glanced at Chandra, who looked as puzzled as I felt, then back to the screen. "I'm afraid not. Who is she?"

"She's Dr. Fevre's assistant. His intern, or whatever they call them at the university. He's mentioned her, Peggy something. She might know."

"I'm sure you're right. Can you give us a number for her?"

"No. I have no idea, but she must have one. Everybody does."

There was nothing for it but to screen the university and ask for Dr. Fevre.

A pleasant female voice said, "Anatomy." The face on the screen was quite pretty, youthful and framed in dark curls.

I tried to sound both pleasant and important. "May I speak to Dr. Fevre?"

"He's not here, and I can't say when he'll be back." When I didn't speak, Peggy something added, "Shall I put you on his message board?"

"That shouldn't be necessary. Do you have his eephone number?"

"It's off, I'm sure. He often turns it off when he's busy."

"I'd like the number, even so. If it's off, I'll screen him again later."

The pretty crimson mouth tried not to smile; Peggy was

enjoying this. "I'm afraid I can't give that out, sir. May I ask who's screening?"

I would have tried to look less like a reclone if only I had known how. I didn't think she had made me yet, but I couldn't be sure. "My name is Smithe, Doctor-ah . . . ?"

"Pepper. I'm Professor Margaret Pepper."

I gave her the most charming smile I could manage. "My name is Ern A. Smithe, Professor Pepper. That's Smith with a final E. I'm looking for Dr. Fevre on behalf of Adah Fevre, Dr. Fevre's wife. She's bedridden. No doubt you know."

It brought a smile from Prof. Pepper. "His estranged wife."

At that moment I knew exactly how a bloodhound feels when it catches the scent of blood. Trying hard not to sound as eager as I felt, I said, "Correct. It concerns Chandra, their daughter. You're aware that Dr. Fevre has a daughter?"

"Yes, certainly."

"Is he on that island?"

"Lichholm?" Peggy Pepper hesitated. "I wouldn't know. I suppose it's possible, but in winter . . ."

"No doubt it's unpleasant." I was trying hard not to sound as pleased as I felt. "Still, if his research required it I would think he might go there, even in winter. Do you know if he has a flitter?"

Pretty Professor Pepper looked a trifle startled. "Why, no. No, he doesn't . . . not as far as I know. I feel sure that would be terribly expensive."

I said, "Thank you very much; you've been most helpful. You're Professor Margaret Pepper? Have I got that right?"

"Yes. The next time Dr. Fevre checks in with me, I'll tell him you screened."

When I had thanked Prof. Peggy Pepper and terminated the

screen, I turned to Chandra. "I hope you found that as interesting as I did."

She shook her head, making her braids dance. "I don't think I understood much at all. Could he really fly there in a flitter? Get to the island?"

"If half a dozen cadavers would suffice, I don't see why not. It might require a good deal of range, but since we don't know where this island is I don't really know. The flitter might have, ah, sanitary conveniences."

"Sure, a pee-pot or something."

"Sleeping quarters would be nice, too. If, ah—"

A new voice, low, female, and energetic, announced, "I'm coming too! You have to take me." Adah Fevre wore tough-looking green halfpants and a shining, soft blouse whose colors depended on the angle at which the light struck it; turn a little, and yellow vanished where scarlet or crimson appeared. The biggest butcher knife I have ever seen had been pushed through her belt without a sheath. "Do you have a lot of money?"

I tried to say hell no, but it came out polite: "I'm afraid not."

"Neither do I. We'll have to charter a boat. Do you know how to handle one?"

I shook my head.

"Well then, is there another reclone at that library of yours who might help us?"

"I don't know. I haven't been there long enough to get acquainted. Do you know of anyone?"

Adah Fevre shook her head.

"Then what about a fully human? That might be better."

"Like me? It would be worse, Mr. Smithe. Much, much worse, since both of us would try to command. And no, I don't know of anyone who might be of help." Adah hesitated. "I haven't the least idea, but I'll try to think of someone. Meanwhile you really ought to get acquainted with the other reclones at that library of yours."

"I certainly will. Have we got enough money to charter a boat?"

"I think so, but we can steal one if we don't." Adah Fevre's hand found the ponticwood handle of her butcher knife. "Piracy's traditional in my family; I'm a Morgan on my mother's side." For a moment she smiled savagely at her daughter. "You must try to remember that, Chandra, and tell your brats."

Adah's attention returned to me. "I have no idea what my husband's up to, but whatever it is we'll find out and put a stop to it."

On my way back to the library, I thought of a cartoon I'd seen somewhere. A little boy was telling his dog about all the arrangements his parents had made for a long family vacation. There were twenty or thirty at least, all the way from a neighbor who had promised to take in the paper to a service that was supposed to have someone trustworthy come into the house to water his mother's African violets and dust. Through all that, his pet thought over and over: *Who's going to feed the dog?*

In this case that could be dismissed, I felt sure. Mrs. Heuse would, just as she must have before. But with Adah Fevre gone, would a simple bowl of dog food or table scraps be enough? It seemed almost certain that the dog had once been hers. Had she really forgotten it completely?

I worried over another question, too. What do you call it when a man sets out to avenge his own murder? *Suicide* works, but I did not care for that one.

The Spice Grove Public Library had boasted of having no less than twenty-six reclones of (somewhat) famous writers, including me. The Polly's Cove Public Library had a scant six. Nigel Hart was a military historian. Hans von Rhein had written texts on horology. The other four were just names to me, and nothing in their conversation at dinner that night—or at least nothing in the snatches that I could overhear—told me what they had written about. Even so I learned their names, and noted them down on a scrap of paper as soon as I got the chance.

The library's screens were supposed to be out of bounds for us; but when it was closed and all the doors were locked, there were only three 'bots to keep me from using a screen. As soon as a patrolling 'bot had passed, I typed in the name of one of my new teammates.

The Rudiments of Sailing, Building a Small Racing Sloop, A Lifetime's Slavery to the Wind, Let's Revive the Topsail Schooner . . .

On to the next. *Primitive Navigation, Polynesians and Phoenicians, A Deep Breath and a Big Stone, Lost at Sea* . . . That seemed promising. I made a check mark beside the author's name: Audrey Hopkins.

A quarter of an hour later, I went looking for her. She was already asleep, and I was tempted to wake her up but on further reflection that seemed like a bad idea. Dog tired, I turned in myself instead.

Next morning I was able to get a seat next to her at breakfast. I had rehearsed the first few lines.

"May I sit here, Ms. Hopkins? And introduce myself? I'm Ern Smithe—that's Smith with an E at the end—and I wrote mysteries. I wanted to tell you how much I enjoyed *The Boats of the Yerba Buena*."

She had a charming smile. "Did you really read that? I'm flattered."

"I hoped you would be." I smiled back. "Yes, I did. It's a fine book and an unusual book. One usually finds men writing about men's adventures, while women write about love affairs, gowns, balls, and intrigues."

"But I wrote about men's adventures?"

"No. Even though that would be sufficiently unusual. You wrote about men's misadventures. Far from a common topic, even from men."

The smile again. "Somehow, we women rarely make it into the lifeboats. I can scarcely imagine a lifeboat full of us."

Play long enough and you've got to get lucky. It had been a favorite saying of the first me's father; I could almost see him smiling down from wherever. I said, "I can't offer that, but I'm going to come close. Two women, a girl, the boat, and me. Do you get checked out a lot?"

The smile faded. "Must I tell you?"

"No. I have no authority, meaning no way verifying your veracity." I paused, as though composing a truly wonderful tale. "On one unforgettable occasion—here I give a single example when I might give you several—I was checked out by two patrons at once. It was the wonder of the Spice Grove Public Library and remains so to this day, but what outsider would believe it?"

One shapely feminine eyebrow challenged me. "And they credited you for both?"

"They did. Circumstances demanded it and so did I. My patrons on that well-remembered occasion, should you care to investigate further, were an heiress, Ms. Colette Coldbrook, and a plainclothes detective named Payne. I have reason to doubt that you frequently encounter checkouts like that here in Polly's Cove."

She shook her head; the gesture held a charm I could not have explained in a week. "I've been checked out twice in the past four years, Mr. Smithe."

I'm not good at sympathetic, but I tried when I said, "A checkout every two years is better than nothing."

"But not much better; I'm well aware of it."

Taking a deep breath and picking my words, I told her, "I can arrange for you to be checked out today, Ms. Hopkins. I'm not boasting; I can do it and I will do it if you want me to. I could— only to be fair I ought to tell you about the circumstances first."

"You're serious?"

I nodded, striving to look as serious as a judge. "Completely."

"Call me Audrey, please."

I said, "I'm dead serious, Audrey. Absolutely serious. This isn't a joke and it isn't some kind of swindle."

"Then why aren't you checked out yourself?"

"I am. I was sent back to the library to find—all right if I say 'recruit'?—somebody like you. My patron and I had no particular person in mind. I was to find the right person."

"As you have?" There was no smile.

"I hope so. If you'll agree, you and I will visit the waterfront and charter a fishing boat. We'll charter the one called the *Three Sisters*, if we can get it."

"This is real?" Audrey's hopeful voice was deeper than many men's.

"Very. We're not treasure hunters. We'll be looking for my patron's husband, Dr. Barry Fevre. He's been away from home for seven years, roughly." For a few seconds I stopped talking to think. When Audrey didn't speak, I said, "Mrs. Fevre sometimes says twelve years. That may be a lie or an error, or some sort of subjective truth; I wish I knew which."

Audrey was silent, so I added, "He may have gone to look for cadavers. We think that's the most probable reason."

Her eyes went wide.

"He teaches anatomy to medical students. He needs cadavers for them to dissect, and they're hard to find."

"You said you wrote mysteries." There was a half smile now. "Did you ever write one like this?"

"Absolutely not, nor am I spinning one now. If anyone can be said to be spinning anything, it's Dr. Fevre." I paused in case she had a question, then posed one of my own. "Have you decided?"

"No. I take it we're going off to look for him in this boat you mentioned."

"We are. That will be Mrs. Fevre, the Fevres' daughter Chandra, and me. I'd like to have you along as well. It will be a cold voyage in winter, and we may end up somewhere in the arctic. There will be carefully rationed food prepared by the boat's galley, freezing winds, and rough seas. I won't lie to you about this."

"*We did seal, we did seal . . .*" Singsong, so soft that I could scarcely make out the words. I pretended that I had heard nothing. After a moment Audrey halted her song to say, "I once crossed the Irish Sea in a sailing canoe, Ern. Did you know that?"

It had been in the author's write-up at the end of *The Boats of the Yerba Buena*; I nodded and said, "Tell me about it."

"I did, it took five days; and when it was finally over I swore I'd never do anything like that again. This isn't like that."

I nodded again.

"For one thing I had a support boat that always kept me in sight. If my canoe had capsized, I would've had a chance of rescue—a slim chance, but a real one. Will we have a support boat?"

I shook my head. "I'm afraid not."

"I didn't think so. May I ask why we want the *Three Sisters?*"

"You may, and I'll be glad to explain everything as soon as we have you checked out."

"Over rum and pineapple juice, Mr. Smithe?"

She had guessed I had money; knowing that made me grin. "You drive a hard bargain, Ms. Hopkins. All right, if you know where we can get them."

I screened Chandra after that. She had been asleep and was still in her flannel nightgown. She told me that her mother had gone back to bed (which I had more than half expected) and that she didn't want to wake her. I told her about Audrey, and she promised to fix it.

Audrey and I chatted a bit after that until a librarian I had not seen before came in to say that a Mrs. Fevre had checked Audrey out and there was someone here who would take her to Mrs. Fevre's home.

"I will in fact take you to Mrs. Fevre's," I said when we were well away from the library. "Only not now. First, we have to find and engage the *Three Sisters*, if we can. Then, rum and pineapple juice. After that, the Fevre house—one of them, anyway."

My final remark hoisted the eyebrows. "Do you really think there's more than one?"

Sometimes I have a hard time sounding completely serious, but it was easy now. "I think there are probably more than two."

We were lucky in the abrupt way that Lady Luck shows up when you are not looking for her. *Three Sisters* was in port and the sim in its screen sounded happy to see us. A look around— as long and nitpicky as I could make it—showed that the boat was every bit as bad as I had expected, and maybe worse. The sim said she would repaint as soon as she got the money, and I told her she would be paid when the trip was over and not before. She had caught on already that this was going to be a lot more than a one-day outing. Up on the bridge she and I fussed over the details, with input from Audrey whenever she felt like it. It ended up like this: A thousand to begin. That would let our new boat clean up and repaint, and more than cover her rental for a week. Three hundred more was to be paid when we sailed, and the rest when we left the boat. That would be a hundred for every day over the first week.

We would sail as soon as we could, provided that the boat was ready—only not until tomorrow at soonest, since all of us would have to pack and we'd have to lay in some supplies. The boat's sim said she'd have some shopping to do, too; also we'd have to allow time for her fresh paint and spar varnish to dry.

When we got away from there, Audrey showed me a little food-and-drink joint on a dark side street. It was called McKean's and was the sort of place that had candles on the table—only not lit for lunch—and a smoky little fire in a stone fireplace. No tablecloths. "You owe me a rum and pineapple juice, Ern. I only hope you've got the money."

"Some. Not enough to hire that boat, but more than enough to buy us drinks."

"And maybe something to eat? I know it's early yet."

I ordered drinks. "We'll eat when we get to the Fevre house. Free there."

Audrey looked thoughtful. "Technically, they don't have to feed me until tonight."

"I believe we may disregard that."

Audrey was quiet until two tall, frosted glasses came; then she asked, "How do you like your drink?"

I wanted to say it tasted like pineapple juice over ice, but "Delicious" seemed more diplomatic.

"You got me checked out, so I ought to have bought; I'm sorry you had to."

"That's quite all right."

"It was my obligation." Audrey paused. "You, however, are obliged to tell me why the boat had to be the *Three Sisters*, and no other. You'll recall that you promised you would over drinks."

"Did I?" I leaned back in my chair. "I wanted to get that boat because Dr. Fevre chartered it originally to take him to Lichholm. It will have firsthand knowledge of those waters, reefs, rocks, beaches, currents, and all the rest. Also it seems probable that he won't try to dodge it if it comes back again, as he might a boat he doesn't know. I'm hoping that he'll stick around to find out why it has returned."

After a moment, Audrey nodded. "That's sensible."

"Thanks." I took a quarter minute to arrange my thoughts. "Lastly, it's a fishing boat, so I knew it would have big refrigerated tanks in the hold. Remember those? They're where the catch goes when the fishermen shake it out of their nets. Those tanks should be just about perfect for cadavers."

"Fresh cadavers, presumably." Audrey shuddered. "They wouldn't want them to rot and stink."

I borrowed her word. "Presumably."

"Lichholm. It means the Isle of Corpses. Did you know that, Ern?"

I nodded. "I did, although I always think of it as Cadaver Island."

"Why would anybody call an island that?"

I shrugged. "I don't know, Audrey. It's something we may find out."

7

CONVERSATIONS

Back when I started that last chapter, I thought I would jump right to the island in this one. Only now I'm not going to. The more I think about what being there was like, the more I think I ought to write a little about how it was for the four of us—especially me—on the boat. Maybe I ought to leave out the seasickness; but all of us got seasick, and once on the first day all four of us were puking over the rail at the same time. If you've been seasick you know how it was, but if you haven't you really can't imagine. The boat keeps jumping around under your feet, and you wish the devil in charge of that were on it with you and you could get your hands around his stinking neck.

Because it never stops. Not ever. Not even for one minute. The boat told me later that it is nowhere near as bad on a big ship because they have fins down under water; those fins are programmed and try to take care of things. Only on a boat as small as ours fins do not work and would cost too much anyway.

The rolling is bad and the pitching is worse. When the boat does both at once, that is the worst of all and so bad I can't describe it. When the rolling and pitching don't make you chuck, you've got your sea legs. All four of us got sea legs eventually, but it seemed like it took two forevers. Audrey got over her seasickness first, and she had never minded being sick and chucking very much because she'd known it was coming, what it was going to be like, and when she'd get over it. She offered up her suffering and sort of went with the flow. On the way back, I tried to do that too.

Chandra got over being sick next, and pretty soon after Audrey. Chandra told me later that she had only chucked three times, and when she'd had stomach flu it had been a whole lot worse. It was two days after that before I got over being sick, and those were two of the longest days in my life.

Finally Adah Fevre got over it, but she took longer than anybody else because she spent so much time in her cabin. She'd wake up and chuck over the side of her bunk, wipe her mouth, and go right back to sleep. It's always bad to be inside in rough weather, and it was worse for Audrey and me because the two of us slept side by side on the floor next to Adah's bunk. When she was sick, we caught as much as we could in a bucket and cleaned up mornings and evenings, washing the bucket, the floor, and everything else, ourselves included, with seawater.

Here I ought to say something about the bunks. They folded up into the wall whenever a fully human was not using them. A fully human made his or hers up—or didn't—and pressed a button, and like magic the bunk disappeared into the wall. It gave fully humans a bit more room for whatever they wanted to do in their cabins.

It would be nice (and easy) to say that Chandra cut out paper dolls or something and mostly left Audrey and me alone except for meals, but it wouldn't be true. Usually Chandra was right in there with us or else pounding on our door, so no sex at all for the first couple of nights. After those nights, we just left our door unlocked all day; then at night we bolted it, and when Chandra beat on it I would whisper through the crack, saying we had been asleep and her mother and Audrey were still asleep, so keep quiet and go away. Most of the time it worked pretty well.

Only one morning it wasn't Chandra pounding on the door, it was Adah. She had gone out leaving Audrey and me alone. As soon as she was gone, we had thrown off our blanket and stripped. I told Adah I slept naked and what did she want? She said she wanted in, so I said, "All right, but you've got to give me a minute to get my clothes on." Then I did, even though Adah kept right on pounding. When I let her in, she yelled, "Where's Chandra?"

Audrey said, "In her room asleep, I imagine. Did you wake up both of us for that?"

Adah said, "You can just get up off that floor and sit down somewhere so you can talk to me."

Audrey shook her head. "I'm not about to stand up in my filmy nonexistent nightgown with dawn coming through the porthole and a man in the room. May I respectfully suggest that you go back to bed and get some sleep? We can talk at breakfast."

"It's morning already," Adah told us. "My daughter spends too much time with you two, and I don't like it."

I said, "You're talking to the wrong people. Do you think we bribe her with steaming creamys? If you want her to stay with you, tell her that."

"You could send her back to me!"

Audrey said, "And what would we do if she disobeyed? Because she would. She'd be sitting in your cabin while you slept for hours. The weather's too bad for her—"

"It was bad enough at home!"

Audrey said, "Was that our fault? You checked me out just a few days ago, and Ern not long before that."

By that time I was looking for the butcher knife. It wasn't in Adah's belt, and I could only hope she hadn't stuck it in the top of her boot.

"You two think I can't do a thing to you!"

I cleared my throat. "You can damage us, you mean. For Audrey's sake, I wasn't going to bring this up; now I've got to. The Polly's Cove Public Library had a copy of me, an old edition they'd owned for years, apparently. You checked him out and damaged him so badly that they had to amputate his arm. Would you like to tell me how that older Ern displeased you?"

Adah only glared at me.

"Whatever it was, you made him pay in spades. There are people who tear pages out of books because they're offended by something the author wrote. Nobody notices the pages are gone until another patron checks out the book and complains, and that may be a year or more after the book was mutilated. My old reclone wasn't—"

"He said Barry was unfaithful!"

I nodded. "I imagine he did. The library did the best they could for him. They may have actually persuaded a surgeon to attend him, but you had hacked his right arm at the shoulder and even an expert surgeon can only do so much. The library has gotten the poor old reclone you'd mutilated new shirts with little magnets glued in place, so that his empty sleeve would stay folded against his chest." There was a pause while I swallowed and tried not to sound as angry as I felt. "That was before somebody cut his throat. I've got on one of the poor guy's old shirts now."

"I came here to talk about Chandra, you fool!"

Audrey jumped in. "I want to talk about her too. She isn't one of us any more than you are. She's fully human, not a library reclone; and if you treat your daughter the way you seem to have treated an earlier copy of Ern, they'll lock you up in an asylum and throw away the key."

There was one of those long silences. Adah glared at us and we gave it back doubled. Finally I told Adah, "Like I said, I'm wearing one of that earlier copy's shirts. If I were to take off this coat, you'd see stains up here near my shoulder—his blood had soaked through his bandages, and bloodstains are damned hard to get out. If Prentice back at the library has half the guts she looks like she has, she'll have hung on to your deposit. Did she?"

Without saying a word, Adah turned on her heel and marched out.

After that Audrey and I got dressed, and in half an hour or so we were leaning over the rail side by side, just a happy couple looking out to sea. Here I ought to explain that we were up on the top deck, on top of the cabins, the bridge, and so on. It was the first time I'd been up there, and I had climbed up because the *Three Sisters* was taking green water over the bow every five minutes or so. If you didn't want to stay in your cabin or get your feet wet, you left the main deck and climbed up on this upper deck quick. Adah had new sea boots and Audrey had old ones, but Chandra and I were stuck with shoes.

To me, the sea is always beautiful. When it is calm, it's like looking at a beautiful woman, a giantess so big that you cannot see all of her at once even though you know she goes on and on, more and more lovely smooth skin with thrilling curves longer than a man's eyes can ever take in. Only when it's as rough as it was then, looking out to sea is like looking at the biggest tiger the world has ever seen, and that tiger is raging, clawing at you, huge white-tipped claws by the thousands and hundreds of thousands crashing against the hull, eager to grab anybody it can reach, pull them overboard, and drown them in a heartbeat. And yet it's still beautiful and I loved it even when it seemed to be trying to sink us. Beauty will do that to you.

Finally Audrey said, "Does this make you think of our patron, Ern?"

"It didn't," I told her, "but now it does. Now it always will, I suppose."

"Sometimes the ocean is lovely and peaceful, and sometimes it's like this. Sometimes it's just a little rough, busy and energetic, with a whistling wind." She waited for me to speak, and when I said nothing she added, "Doesn't that remind you of somebody we know?"

I thought I knew what she was asking. "Perhaps Adah's like that at times, but I've never seen her when she was. Do you know psychology?"

Audrey shook her head. "I'm not superstitious, so no. I haven't studied it because I don't believe a lot of things the psychologists say."

"Neither do I," I said. "I've been wondering whether Dr. Barry Fevre does—or rather, just how much psychology he knows.

Since he's a doctor he must be familiar with the basics, or so it seems to me."

"If he were here now, what would you ask him?"

"Since he's surely had plenty of chances to see that there's something wrong with his wife, why he doesn't get her treatment?" When Audrey made no reply, I finished the thought. "I suppose it's possible he did."

Audrey said something then, but the wind whirled her words away like so many scraps of paper. I got her to repeat them, and she said, "I asked if Chandra would know."

"Maybe she would. I'll find out."

There was another silence. The sun was rising, but it seemed to bring no warmth; its light was fitful and brief, too often stifled by clouds.

"I think you're out to avenge the death of that earlier copy. Am I right, Ern?" Audrey's words were softer than down.

"Yes, I am. I want justice for my earlier self. How did you know?"

"From the way you sounded when you talked about him this morning. Was his throat cut at the Fevres'?"

I shook my head. "He was sitting in the lobby of the library. When I came in, he was all right. Dispirited, and wearing a fire-sale price, but alive. When I went out, he was dead."

"And he was you."

I thought that one over. "In a sense, he was. Yes. We were both Ern A. Smithe, if you like. He was an earlier copy. Of course the original, the manuscript, passed away long before I was published."

"Same here." Audrey was smiling. "My original's been gone for a couple of centuries. How did yours die? Do you know?"

I shook my head. "I have no idea. Cancer or a heart attack, probably. But I really have no idea."

"Mine drowned."

I could only stare at her.

"Another book, of course. I was left on an island in the South Pacific with a few hand tools, a saw and a hatchet, a coil of rope, and so on. I was to build a boat—a vessel of some kind—and sail it back to civilization. There was no cameraman with me. I just set the timer and aimed the camera so I'd be in the picture, working or whatever. Roasting a fish." Audrey smiled. "That made a good picture, and there were quite a few good fish to spear, too."

"Did your boat sink?"

She shook her head. "I built a raft. That was what I'd planned all along, although I didn't tell anyone. I felled trees of the right size, trimmed off limbs, dragged the trunks to the beach, and all the rest of it. I built my raft where it floated at high tide but lay on the beach at low tide. That was when I worked on it, mostly."

I nodded to show I understood.

"A storm—a hurricane—was the chief risk. I knew that. You don't get them often in the South Pacific, but if one came . . ."

"It sounds terribly risky."

"It was. Riskier than I had realized. Lonelier too. I started talking to myself, and I still do it now and then."

I said, "I've never noticed."

"It's mostly when I'm alone, or when I'm trying to do something really difficult."

Mostly to keep things rolling, I said, "That can't have been the first time you were on your own."

Audrey shrugged. "Of course I'd been alone on a lot of one-woman voyages, but building the raft while foraging for food took longer than the longest of those solo adventures. I lost weight I couldn't afford to lose, and—"

I said, "Wait a minute. When was your last scan?"

"About a year before that. Let me think." Audrey was quiet for a few seconds. "Eleven months before I went to the island. You're wondering how I know all this."

"Of course I am."

"I found a book-length biography of myself while I was on loan to the library in Port Purity. It was detailed and quite accurate, and made interesting reading. There were a few trivial errors, but nothing major."

"You were sending in reports from the island?"

"Screening them, yes. Reports and pictures. The last report—the book gave the whole thing, word for word—said my raft was breaking up in a rough sea. No hurricane, just six-foot waves." She shrugged. "I was never heard from again."

I considered that. "They must have had tissue samples, or blood or something. They recloned you, after all."

Audrey shook her head. "Only my DNA on file. That's all they need. Let's talk about something else, Ern."

I agreed, but we did not. I was a little embarrassed and felt sure I'd put my foot in it. Maybe she was, too. However that was, we just stood together at the railing watching the waves and enjoying each other's company—or anyhow I enjoyed hers and I like to think she enjoyed mine.

"This is a lot smoother than the one that broke up my raft," Audrey said after we had stood there staring out to sea for five or ten minutes.

I nodded. It was calmer now, almost like glass.

"Can you see that?" She pointed. "Down there."

I stared. "The big black thing? It's longer than this boat."

"Yes. That's its back."

"Is it a whale?"

"I hope not. They attack boats like this—boats smaller than they are—sometimes."

That hit so hard that I could barely keep my voice from trembling. "Why would they do that?"

Audrey shrugged. "Whales were hunted for centuries. First with harpoons that seamen threw from small boats, then with harpoons shot from a deck gun. We don't hunt them anymore, as far as I know." She was silent for a moment; then she added, "We've stopped hunting them, but they haven't forgotten."

We were silent for quite a while after that, each of us wrapped in our own thoughts.

When the wind picked up and a fair-sized vessel with sails came into view, Audrey told me what boats with its rig were called and how they were operated.

After we had watched it for ten minutes or so, I went down to the bridge; touching the screen there brought up the sim. She looked as jaunty as ever, with her white cap tilted a bit to one side and a crisp, clean uniform. I told her I wanted to borrow binoculars or a telescope. Anything like that.

"There's a lugger at one o'clock, sir. Is that what you want to see?"

I didn't know what a lugger was, but I nodded.

"I can show you better than binoculars could." She faded as she spoke. Here came a sea view, bringing an explanation of what I was seeing. The sailing vessel I had spotted got bigger and bigger as I watched. It looked twice as big as our boat, with a wooden hull that had been patched in places and two masts, the foremast raked forward and the aft raked back. Both masts carried brown lug sails, and both lug sails were reefed. I would have said it was going to go down any minute, but the crew moving around on deck did not look panicky.

I asked the screen if it could identify the boat, and got the sim again. "No, sir. Name unknown to me and none painted on the hull."

"Is that the boat that took Dr. Barry Fevre away when he sailed with you?"

There was a brief delay before the sim said, "Looks like it, sir, but I can't be certain."

I wanted to tell her to go closer to the lugger, but it seemed obvious that I couldn't board it in this weather. I wouldn't be able to learn much by shouting questions at the skipper either, and a vessel as primitive as the lugger wouldn't have anything remotely like a screen.

Thinking about all that I said, "Follow that boat!" It wasn't until I had gotten it out that I realized it was the old, old, "Follow that groundcar!" with a little alteration to make it fit.

Smiling, the sim touched her cap. "Aye aye, sir!"

I hadn't been sure she'd do what I said, but in a moment I could feel our boat going around. That brought up a question I'd been wanting to ask. I knew it was kind of foolish, but I was pretty sure the boat was not going to laugh at me for asking it. "Will I ever get to see the other two sisters?"

The sim never turned a hair. "Perhaps, sir. When they're in port." She paused to let me comment, then added, "They are the *Mermaid* and the *Lady Luck*, sir."

I wanted to know more, but I couldn't think of a good way to phrase my question. Maybe if I had just blurted it out my conditioning would have fixed it. (It does that for me just about always. I have to talk the way the first Ern A. Smithe wrote exposition; I'm pretty sure I've told you about that already.)

Audrey pointed when I got up on the top deck again. "Have you seen that sailboat, Ern?"

I said I had. "I went down to ask our boat about it, and she showed me a close-up in her screen. It might be the boat that took Dr. Fevre off. My guess is that it is."

"I hadn't noticed it until we turned toward it. That was your doing, wasn't it? Giving orders down there on the bridge?"

I nodded.

The wind was blowing too hard for me to hear Chandra's boots on the steps; I didn't realize that she had climbed up to join us until she said, "Are we going to catch it, Mr. Smithe?"

I looked around and asked how her mother was.

"She's gotten all quiet again. Only the first time, she tore into me so bad I ran outside in my PJ's. She probably thought I went out on deck like that, but I didn't."

"Good!" That was Audrey.

"I ducked into that little cabin back over the engine." Chandra grinned. "It sounds pretty bad back there, but maybe I could get used to it. After I'd been in there awhile it didn't bother me much."

"People must sleep in there sometimes, when they have a lot of fishermen on board."

"Yeah. You know what I did?"

Audrey smiled. "I can't imagine. What was it?"

"There's no furniture in there to hide behind or anything, so

I climbed into a top bunk and reached out to push the button. It shut right up with me inside."

I said, "You could have suffocated."

"Nah. Push against it, and it opens up a little. After a while I did that until I could reach out and push the button again. Then it opened right up. That's when I went back to our cabin to get my clothes. Mother was awake, only just lying in her bunk staring up at the one on top of hers. You know how she does."

I nodded.

"So I didn't say anything. I put these on fast and came out on deck. Then I saw you guys up here."

Audrey said, "I'm glad you did. We wouldn't want you to get washed over the rail."

"It's not that rough."

"Not now, but it wouldn't have to get much rougher. It could happen, and it would happen fast."

Chandra stared at her, then nodded.

"I've sailed a lot. I crossed the Atlantic, alone, in a little yawl; and once I set out to circumnavigate the globe in a sloop. I put a world of water behind me before I was captured by pirates in the Indian Ocean."

I added, "She crossed the Irish Sea all by herself in a canoe."

"I didn't know." Chandra sounded apologetic.

Audrey said, "What I'm trying to get at is that somebody your age going to sea had better listen to anybody who's willing to teach her. You can't know too much, and the smaller your boat the smarter you've got to be. Do you know how I died? The original me?"

Slowly, Chandra shook her head. "I never even thought about it."

"I drowned when my raft fell apart. Maybe I'll tell you more about that sometime, but I really don't enjoy talking about it."

"Were you alone on the raft?"

Audrey nodded.

"You liked that. Liked being alone."

"Sometimes I did. Yes." Audrey fell silent, and I wished I could hear what she was thinking.

Chandra said, "I like being alone, too. Sometimes."

Before the silence became awkward, I said, "You must have friends at school."

"Some." Chandra shrugged. "Friends, but I'm not really tight with anybody. We're friends in the morning, only not after lunch. You know how I mean?"

I nodded.

Audrey said, "There are people who'll work without being told, and not talk unless you want to talk too. But not a lot of them. Really, very few."

There was more conversation before we caught up to the lugger, but I don't remember everything and none of it was all that interesting.

What happened when we caught up was somebody on the lugger shouted, "Permission to come aboard?"

You would have thought our boat would have asked one of us if it was all right, but it did not unless maybe it asked Adah Fevre. It just shot a fishing net out to the lugger. I suppose it was thirty or forty meters, but the net reached and there was enough left over for the lugger's crew to tie it down some way.

A man jumped on it a lot quicker than I would have and started climbing across. Of course the net sagged into the water between our boat and the lugger, and for quite a bit of that distance his head went under every time a wave hit. He stayed with it though; I like to think I'm tough, but I had to admit that he was a lot tougher than I am.

Writing like this, it can be pretty close to impossible to tell about a certain thing so that it reads the way the thing actually was, and this is one of them. When the man finally scrambled up onto the main deck, oilskins and all and everything dripping wet, he saw us and I saw him. As soon as I did I knew who he was. I'd only gotten a glimpse of him in the library, but I knew anyway. I whispered to Audrey, "Adah's husband!"

Half a minute later he was standing on the top deck with us; he stuck out his hand and said, "Barry Fevre."

8

To Lichholm

If there had been time to think, I might not have taken his hand; after all, I thought he had cut the old me's throat. That was bad, and the way I saw it he was certain-sure to try for mine the first good chance he had, which was a whole bunch worse. Thing was, I didn't have time to think; and the way he'd crossed on the net through that wild sea, climbing from one boat to the other, was the bravest thing I'd ever seen. So I shook his hand and said, "I'm Ern A. Smithe, Doctor," the way you do, and introduced Audrey. She gave him her hand and a nice smile, but I felt certain her fingers were crossed.

After that he kissed Chandra's cheek, and said, "Good to see you again, honey."

She sort of nodded, he straightened up, and Audrey said, "You must be freezing."

He shivered. "I am. If there's a warm cabin in there . . . ?"

I said, "Sure." My brain had caught up to what was going on by then, which was that it had two big facts to wrestle with. First, I believed he'd cut the throat of the old man who had been an earlier edition of me. Second, I didn't know that for certain. It seemed likely as hell because he'd been right there. But why would he do it? Motive, means, and opportunity; from what I've read, those are the three legs of a criminal investigation. Dr. Fevre had the second and the third, but that first one looked terribly iffy. He would have had to know Adah'd checked out the old me because she was looking for him. He'd also have to know, or anyway believe, that the old me had found out quite a bit. But—and this was one hell of a big glitch—he couldn't know that Adah had cut off the old me's arm and returned him to the library, which meant the old me was no danger to him anymore. No more motive, which made Doc Fevre's guilt pretty damned unlikely.

It gets worse. He couldn't help but know that he could've bought the old me for peanuts. The price had been hanging around the poor old me's neck, and for a tenured professor it wasn't much more than pocket money. If he bought him, he could cut his throat or burn him, or just shove him off a nice high cliff; and there would be no trouble about it. It would be perfectly legal. As it was, the library's lobby was full right then, there were people all around. Sure, maybe nobody would notice, but it was more likely that somebody would. Suppose it got out? Wouldn't there be questions at the faculty meeting? Lots of questions from his students, too, after his sabbatical was over?

So why not buy the old me—dirt cheap like I said—off him in private, and hand him over to the students to dissect? You needed bodies for that, but did they have to be fully humans? Leaving aside facial details, there isn't a broken token's worth of difference between a reclone and a fully human. How could there be?

Could I have heaved Dr. Fevre over the side some dark night? I'd seen glowing things down there that were too big to be human and too much like humans to be fish. So if I grabbed him when he wasn't expecting it . . . Only I needed to know one hell of a lot more before I tried anything like that. You can see why I was thinking so fast that smoke might come out of my ears any minute.

Right then Audrey told him, "We've got two warm cabins with chairs and so on. Ern and I sleep beside your wife's bed— Adah Fevre's your wife, isn't she?"

He nodded.

"She has one and Chandra has the other. If you'd like to see your wife now . . . ?"

Dr. Fevre shook his head. "I need to dry off first. Dry off and get warm. Can I strip somewhere private, wrap myself in a blanket, and put my clothes in the dry washer?"

Chandra said, "I'll do that, and you can change in my cabin."

So we went down to the main deck and I fetched one of the spare blankets. Then Audrey and I went back up onto the top deck, leaving Dr. Fevre alone in Chandra's cabin, with Chandra waiting outside. When he was dressed again, Chandra came up and got us. We found him nice and dry, sitting in one of her bolted-down chairs and sipping kafe.

He raised the cup. "I ordered this. I don't think my wife will object."

Audrey said, "I'm sure she won't. Order something to eat, too, if you want it." By then the *Three Sisters* had begun pitching hard as well as rolling; so maybe I ought to explain that the kafe cups had lids with slots you could sip out of. Dr. Fevre did it a lot smoother than I would have; you could see he was an old sailor.

"I took a shower, too, to rinse off the seawater." He waited for one of us to say something. "I tried not to use much fresh water, desalinization should take care of my gallon or so, and we ought to reach Lichholm in a couple of days. There's plenty of fresh water there."

That one surprised me. I said, "You knew we were going to Lichholm?"

He nodded. "It seemed a safe assumption. I screened this boat hoping to get her to come there and pick me up, and found out that she'd been chartered." He waited, and when I didn't say anything he added, "Her destination was confidential. What wasn't confidential was the name of the person who had chartered her."

"Your wife."

"Yes, Adah. It wasn't hard to guess her destination, or that she had competent friends who were handling things for her."

Audrey said, "We're reclones, Ern and I. I feel sure you know."

He shrugged. "Of course, but there was no reason to bring it up."

"Your wife checked Ern out of the library and enlisted his help, and he talked her into checking me out too."

Dr. Fevre smiled. "You're in his debt."

"Yes, but in hers as well. . . ." Audrey let it trail off. "She's my patron. May I ask why you don't live with her?"

I tried to change the subject, but Dr. Fevre waved it away. "I'll explain."

He turned to Chandra. "I meant to get you alone and tell you about this, honey; but I might as well do it now. Not many people ask, but I tell anybody who does."

Chandra nodded, looking so uncomfortable I expected her to run off.

"Your mother has an emotional disorder. It causes her to alternate, without warning or pause, from wild elation to severe depression. I know you can't know a great deal about psychology. Nor do I, for that matter."

He turned to Audrey and me. "Do either of you?"

I shook my head.

Audrey said, "No. Nothing, really."

"I have consulted psychologists, experienced people who have dealt with many cases of this type. It is, as I told you, an emotional disorder." He took a deep breath. "That means it's not a mental disorder. Neither psychologists nor psychiatrists are permitted to treat sane individuals who do not desire treatment. I've tried repeatedly to persuade Adah to get treatment. She insists there is nothing wrong with her."

Audrey looked at me before she spoke. "Ern and I are checked out of the Polly's Cove Public Library, both of us. Chandra came for us, but officially it was your wife who checked us out; that means she's our patron."

"Which is why you two are on this boat. I understand."

Audrey wasn't finished. "As library resources, we're obligated to inform our patron. We don't have to mop floors or load dirty dishes into the sterilizer; but when our patron travels, she's entirely within her rights to require us to accompany her."

Dr. Fevre smiled. "And you do your duty, just as I strive to do mine."

"I said we weren't required to load dishes. We aren't, but we generally try to be helpful within reason. For one thing, it looks good for us if we're checked out a lot. It doesn't have to be different patrons. If one patron checks us out four times in a year, our record shines. Do you know what I mean?"

Dr. Fevre said, "Certainly."

I stuck my oar in. "There's a lady who checks me out once a year, every year."

Audrey said, "That alone makes Ern pretty solid. It's when a year goes by and nobody checks a certain resource out that she looks bad."

I said, "Now you know where we stand. You've been to Lichholm. Several times, I believe. We haven't, and I don't think your wife knows anything about it."

Chandra put in, "I don't either."

Audrey said, "You're going there on your sabbatical, and I'm reasonably sure you've been there before. Since Ern and I know nothing about the place, how about filling us in?"

"Gladly." Dr. Fevre smiled. "Lichholm is a small island off the northernmost coast, not far from the Arctic Circle. I don't know the population but it cannot be much more than a thousand, and may be less. Some of the world's richest fishing grounds lie to the southeast, and nearly all of the men fish."

For a moment he fell silent.

"Their island came to my attention originally because of its ice caves."

I suppose my eyes opened wider or I sat up straighter or something. Whatever it was, it made Dr. Fevre chuckle. "That's right, caverns of ice. Caverns in a glacier. Very extensive and very beautiful caves of crystal-clear ice, although to see them you have to bring a flashlight or a lantern. Their existence is almost unknown to the rest of the world, but I have explored them. I'll be delighted to show them to you when we get to Lichholm—assuming that you'd like to see them."

Very truthfully I said I certainly would.

Audrey nodded, and Chandra exclaimed, "Me too!"

"In that case I must warn you"—Dr. Fevre was still smiling gently—"that those ice caverns contain thousands of corpses."

Audrey gasped loudly enough for me to hear her.

"For generations, the inhabitants of the island have interred their dead in the ice caves, where the intense cold preserves them perfectly."

Audrey said, "Now I understand the name of the island. I've been wondering about that."

Dr. Fevre nodded. "It makes perfect sense, when one thinks about it. If a young woman wishes to see what her great-grandmother looked like, she can be taken there and shown. Or suppose a man is away from the island when his wife dies of a fever. When he returns, he can be shown his wife's body. He knows then that she is in sober fact dead, and that she did not die by violence."

I said, "What about the treasure? Why not tell us about that?"

Dr. Fevre started to speak, but closed his mouth firmly before the first word came out. Audrey stared at me.

"I saw a map of that island once," I said. "There was a star on it in a little rectangle. It seemed pretty clear that whatever the rectangle represented was the reason the map had been made. When I saw it, I had no idea who had drawn it, but I believe I could offer a really good guess now."

Audrey and I waited for Dr. Fevre to speak; when he said

nothing Audrey turned to me. "We've stopped pitching. Have you noticed, Ern? Almost stopped, anyhow."

There was a lot more talk, but I have given all the most interesting stuff. When Dr. Fevre's clothes were dry, he and Chandra went off to visit Adah, and Audrey went out on deck again. I knew she expected me to join her, but I went up onto the bridge for a few minutes first.

When I came down again and found Audrey on the main deck, she asked, "Are you taking questions?"

I shrugged. "Depends on what they are. I don't know everything anyway."

"What do you know about the star on that map you saw? Does it mean treasure?"

I shook my head. "I've no idea what it means. Your guess is as good as mine."

"Then how about this one?" She lowered her voice. "What do you think of Dr. Barry Fevre?"

I shrugged again. "He's handsome, brave, smooth, and plausible. Maybe slick, too. I haven't quite made up my mind about slick."

"Was he telling the truth? About those ice caves, I mean."

"Probably. I don't know."

"Does our patron trust him?"

I shook my head.

"You know she doesn't, or you just think she doesn't?"

"Now you're splitting hairs," I told Audrey. "I'm reasonably confident that she doesn't. Let's say she may trust him sometimes, but not most of the time."

Audrey pulled the wool coat Adah Fevre's money had bought her a little bit tighter. "Do you?"

"Of course not."

"I don't either. It's just a feeling."

I said, "For me, it's more than a feeling. For one thing, he lied when he told us he expected to find his wife on this boat. He would never have climbed across on that net if he had. From his point of view, Adah's going to complicate the hell out of things."

"He was expecting someone else?"

I nodded. "Absolutely."

"Who? Do you know?"

"Not for sure, but I can make a good guess—a lady called Peggy Pepper. Professor Peggy Pepper, if you like P's or want to be formal. Black hair, clear complexion, and quite attractive, facially at least. I've never met her, but I screened her once. Good voice, too."

"I've been married twice and I still didn't guess." Audrey made a joke of it. "Silly me!"

I said, "A good-looking man, barely middle-aged, has money and an attractive but emotionally disturbed wife. He leaves her, which I find understandable; but he never comes back for a visit. Not in years. Their twelve-year-old daughter hardly knows what he looks like." I paused, staring out at the dark and rolling sea and thinking about the old Ern A. Smithe, his bowed shoulders, thin gray hair, and despondent face; someday soon that would be me.

Trying to shake the thought off, I said, "You can bet the rent that Dr. Barry Fevre's got somebody else. Maybe two or three somebodys, but one for sure."

Audrey was a nice distraction, linking arms and pressing herself against me. "I'm surprised he doesn't divorce Adah."

I said, "There'll be a reason for that, too. I'm not going to guess because it could be any of a dozen things."

Audrey nodded. "Chandra, to begin with. His wife might get custody, although with an emotional illness . . ."

"Doubtful, I agree. He'd almost certainly get custody, which he may not want; but it's probably something else. If a wife dies without a will, her husband gets her property. I've never gotten the impression there was a great deal, but she rents her house and pays her bills—although her housekeeper may be writing the actual checks—and has done it for years. So it's quite possible that there's a lot more money than I would guess."

"What else?"

"He may not want to marry the lovely Peggy, or anybody. A living wife's the perfect excuse."

"I'd think she'd pressure him to get a divorce."

I said, "Perhaps she does, but look at it! His wife's chronically ill and he divorces her and walks away. How would that go over at the faculty meeting? As things are, he's standing loyally by her as far as they know."

Audrey nodded.

"Here's another one. There's a dark secret in his past. Let's say he murdered another fully human ten or fifteen years ago. The fact is known to his wife. He, knowing his wife, feels sure she'll go straight to the police if he files for divorce."

Audrey snapped her fingers. "Wait a minute! He said that when he screened, this boat told him she was chartered. She wouldn't tell him where she was going, but she told him who had chartered her."

I nodded. "You're right, that's what he said."

"Then he would've known his wife was on board!"

I shook my head. "He would if it were true, but it sounded terribly unlikely to me. If the charter were confidential, wouldn't the name of the person—or entity, it might be a company or even some government agency—be confidential, too? Say that I'm going on a terribly private errand. I tell you that you mustn't tell anyone what it is, but it's all right if you tell them that I've gone on a very confidential private errand. Does that sound sensible?"

"I see what you mean."

"So I asked the sim about it. She said no, she just told people she wasn't available. Not why, not even how long, since she couldn't know that with much certainty. Just unavailable."

It was late afternoon before we sighted Lichholm. If the North Atlantic had been quiet and the sun bright, I would have seen it a lot sooner. As it was, it didn't first appear as a tiny dot on the horizon and slowly grow, the sort of thing you read about in travel books. By the time I noticed it—a white peak rising above roaring, white-maned waves—it was already near enough for me to make out a few details. I know how silly this sounds, but my first thought was *The Snow Giants' Castle*. When the first me had been a little kid, some grown-up had given that first me a big, rolled-up picture map of Fairyland. It was supposed to be about fairies, but the biggest thing on it was the Snow Giants' Castle, way back at the back and high up in the mountains. It was twilight in Fairyland, and that picture map gave me the impression that it was always twilight there. A few years later I read about perilous seas in fairylands forlorn and thought yeah, I know about those. Now I felt that I was on one.

Lichholm was a mountain—one big mountain, wide but not very steep—rising out of those perilous seas. A lot of the mountains Arabella and I had seen when we flew in Colette Coldbrook's yellow flitter were snowcapped, and they had been majestic and beautiful. So was this, and more if anything. Lichholm's snowcap ran down to the water, snow on the land and so much snow on the roofs of the houses that I could barely make them out. I wouldn't have noticed them at all if it had not been for the dirty gray smears of smoke that rose from their chimneys until they were whipped away by the wind. Just a couple of days ago, when I was fooling around on one of the screens, I came across a song about whaling; it said, "The king of that country is a fierce Greenland bear." You could sing the same thing about Lichholm. You'd think there was nothing there for bears to eat; but they ate seals and fish, mostly, and once in a while a seabird or one of us.

9

The Only Village on
Corpse Island

When we tied up in Lichholm's little harbor next day, the
lugger was already there. That surprised me; I thought
we would make better time than a fishing boat with sails
could. The bottom fell out of my surprise when a second lugger
rounded the point, giving me a good laugh at my own expense.

Both these luggers were fishing boats, the ancestors of the
Three Sisters. Later I found out there were more than a dozen of
them, all about the same size, all with small engines they rarely
used, and all spreading lug sails on two masts.

The gray smoke and the name of the island had led me to
expect something pretty grim, but the village looked clean
and bright thanks to the new-fallen snow. As far as I could see,
there were no big houses and no big stores, no big buildings of
any kind. There wasn't a whole lot of money around here, in
other words. Just about all the houses were cottages, with steep
roofs that had lofty attics under them. It was all one room up in
those attics sometimes, or maybe two or three attic rooms with
slanted ceilings—take your pick. When a thing's simple enough

it can be hard for it to look old, and that was how it was with those cottages. Unpainted stone walls and gray slates instead of shingles. Stone was cheap here, but wood was for boats and maybe furniture—only there wasn't really enough for either one; more wood had to be brought up from the south. The shops I saw had no window displays to show what they sold. You knew they were shops from the weathered signs hung out front. A needle stuck into a spool of thread is one I remember. Another was a cow's horn with white foam dripping from the big end; it meant the shop sold ale. From what I've said, you can probably tell I kind of liked the place; I would have liked it a lot more if the people hadn't stared so long at strangers like me.

Dr. Fevre was boarding with a family in the village, but they didn't have room for all four of us. They asked around and eventually Audrey and I landed with an old couple named Eiriksdatter. The old folks had six kids, but their kids were grown-ups now, with little stone cottages and big families of their own. The boys were fishermen, all four of them; and none had drowned. Mr. and Mrs. Eiriksdatter sounded proud and happy when they told us about that; it seemed like a good many fishermen drowned. Later on I noticed that when the old woman talked about it she said it like I wrote it: "Not one has drowned." The old man never corrected her, but he said, "None have drowned yet." It makes a real big difference.

We got the kids' old rooms, of course. They were up under the roof and pretty small, so we never did much more than sleep there. The four boys had slept two to a bed; one room went to Adah and another to Chandra. Adah's was bigger and had a window, plus plenty of room for Audrey and me to sleep alongside her bed. We pretended to be a little edgy about having to undress in the same little room. Maybe we fooled the old people, but I could see that Adah and Chandra were not taken in for a minute.

After dinner on the first night, while the old man dozed and his wife did the dishes with a little help from Chandra, I bided my time until Adah went up to bed; call it fifteen or twenty minutes. Then I whispered to Audrey, "You ask me a lot of questions, how about if I ask you one?"

"Sure, if I know the answer."

"Why was Dr. Fevre on that lugger?"

Audrey looked puzzled. "I have no idea. Why don't you ask him?"

"I'm sure he'll have a story. It may be the truth, but I doubt it. He'd tried to charter our boat first. He said so. It wasn't available. What did he want it for?"

"I suppose he wanted it to come here and pick him up. Then it would have brought him back to the mainland."

"To Polly's Cove, that being where it was based."

"Right. To Polly's Cove, where Chandra and his wife live. He teaches in Spice Grove, doesn't he? There's a university there? I think you said that."

I nodded. "He does. But look at the time line. I saw him in the library in Polly's Cove. He walked through the lobby and he may—I said *may*—have cut a tattered old Ern A. Smithe's throat then and there. How long would you say it was between that day, the day I got Adah Fevre to check you out, and the day the *Three Sisters* sailed with you and me on board?"

Audrey took her time. "Close to a week. Maybe a little more."

"I make it six days. I may be off by a day or two, I admit; but

I think six days is right. We were three days on the boat before we sighted the lugger."

"Were we? It seemed longer."

"It was bound to, since we didn't have much to do."

"Bad food didn't help either."

"Right you are. It could be that you're more right than you know. Anyway, we're talking about nine days altogether. Nine days from the time I saw Dr. Fevre in the Polly's Cove Public Library to the time we both saw him cross from boat to boat on a fishing net. Did I say he was brave?"

Audrey nodded. "I think so."

"I hope I did, because he is. He's rich, too. I know he must be because he checked two resource reclones out of the library at the same time."

"Your girlfriends from Spice Grove."

"That's right. Now here's another question. Was the lugger taking him back to the mainland?"

"I see what you mean. It doesn't seem likely, does it?"

I paused, listening to old Mrs. Eiriksdatter chatting with Chandra. "No. No, it doesn't. He would have to come here, presumably with Millie Baumgartner and Rose Romain in tow, and just a day or two later turn around and come back, with or without them."

Audrey said, "I admitted that it doesn't seem likely."

"Agreed, and here's one even less likely. He was on his way back to Polly's Cove, but was perfectly happy when he found out we were going to Lichholm. Wouldn't he have insisted we take him to the mainland first? Or wanted to get back onto his lugger? He was fine with our going to Lichholm. Not one single complaint."

Slowly, Audrey nodded. "He was on his way to Lichholm in that lugger."

"Correct, I'm sure. The question is where are Millie and Rose? My guess is that they were on the lugger with him. Either they stayed below and out of sight, or they were wearing oilskins like Dr. Fevre and the Lichholm men and I wasn't able to spot them among the crew. I think the first one is more likely, but I could be wrong."

"Has the lugger made port yet? Do you know?"

"No, I don't. It could have beaten us, but that's unlikely. Most probably, it was at least a couple of hours behind us. I doubt that it would have tried to tie up after dark, although that, too, is possible. Do you remember the house where Dr. Fevre's staying?"

Audrey nodded.

"Remember where it is?"

"Down at the other end of the street, about as far from the docks as you can get." She paused. "It's almost the last house on the street, and it's a little bigger than the houses on either side of it."

"You've got it, and it seems to me that it's possible that Millie and Rose are in that house with their patron. I'm going down there, keeping my ears open and my mouth shut. If they're there, we may be able to catch a glimpse of them or hear them talking. I know both of them pretty well, and I guarantee that I'll recognize their voices—if they're really there."

Outside, with a cold wind blowing and the snow creaking beneath our feet, Audrey asked, "Why are you so anxious to learn whether your friends are here?"

I told her, "Because I remember Burke and Hare." I was too cold to grin.

"So do I. There was a show about them a few years ago, a musical. I watched it. Do you think Dr. Fevre might do that? Kill people so he can sell their bodies?"

"That depends on what you mean by 'people.'" I tried to make it bitter, but my breath was a plume of steam.

"I see. . . ."

"He couldn't make any money that way—he'd checked them out, so he'd lose his deposits. Still, it might mean keeping his job on the faculty. From what I've read, even a tenured professor can be sent packing, although it's not easy."

Audrey and I had just about reached the cottage where he was staying when she said, "Do we listen at the keyhole?"

I was listening already and motioned for her to keep quiet. One of the male speakers was surely Dr. Fevre; the other was probably his landlord. A third voice sounded like a woman's, and I caught the word "wonderful."

We were nearly at the door by then. After two or three snowy strides more, I knocked.

There was a moment of silence inside, followed by a man's slow steps.

The door opened, and Dr. Fevre's host stared. I said, "May we come in? These coats are warm, but we're freezing anyway."

When he said nothing, I added, "I promise we won't eat much, we've already had dinner."

Rose Romain's slow, breathless voice murmured something I couldn't quite make out. Dr. Fevre called, "Let them come in. They received me hospitably."

I waved Audrey in first and followed her. Before I could sit down, Dr. Fevre said, "Ern, you have no boots. I should've noticed that this afternoon."

I was too busy looking around to answer. A sizable table had been set with five places and wine glasses—most half-full now—and Millie Baumgartner was carrying in a good-sized soup tureen with what looked like a cast-iron lid; she gave me a big smile when she saw us. Our hosts had only four chairs. One belonged to Dr. Fevre, one to the man of the house, and the other two to Rose and Millie. The lady of the house got only a stool, but she managed to find another stool for Audrey and a box for me.

"Soup," Millie told me, taking the iron cover off the tureen. "We all eat right out of this, the way most people did throughout history."

I spooned up some, knowing that it would be delicious. It was.

"French onion," Millie explained. "Most people think there ought to be cheese on top, but that's really Swiss. The French never took to the cheese."

Audrey almost smacked her lips as she asked about the recipe.

"Chop the onions and sauté them in butter," Millie told her. "Add both to beef stock. If you can fry an egg you can make beef stock."

Audrey nodded.

"Add seasoning and stir. Add croutons just before you serve the soup."

"That seasoning is your secret, I'm sure."

Millie laughed. "Not a bit, it's in my book. You will have salted the stock already, so don't add any more salt."

Rose, seated on Dr. Fevre's right, leaned toward him and whispered something that made him smile. I think he pinched her thigh.

"Garlic, thyme, and bay, plus a glass or two of red wine. Just a little dusting of black pepper."

Audrey objected, "It can't be that easy."

"I didn't have everything I needed here, so I did a bit of experimenting."

By the time the fish came in, I had caught on that Rose and Dr. Fevre were holding hands under the table. I'd been worried about Millie and Rose, but it seemed as though Dr. Fevre was treating them a heck of a lot better than library reclones usually get treated. Maybe I ought to say here that Rose was wearing a white silk jacket embroidered with leaves and hanging flowers I think were probably wisteria. She sure as hell had not been slipped into that jacket by the Polly's Grove Public Library.

Audrey asked what the fish was that we were eating and our host told her, but it was one I'd never heard of and I've forgotten it now. It was covered with what Millie told us was just a simple cream sauce with shallots. Hearing that started me wondering just how much of this stuff she had gotten Dr. Fevre to buy her on the mainland, and how much our host and his little bent wife had supplied. Ninety percent and ten would probably cover it.

We talked about food for a few minutes, then I wanted to know when we'd get to see the ice caves.

"Tomorrow, I hope. Come around in the morning." His smile made me nervous.

Audrey said, "Just us? Or your wife and daughter, too?" The

way she said *your wife* tipped me that she knew exactly why Dr. Fevre had checked out Rose Romain.

"I believe we ought to leave that up to them," he told her. It was as smooth as velvet. "They will be more than welcome should they choose to come." He paused, then snapped his fingers. "I'm forgetting something. Mr. Smithe will need boots. What size, Mr. Smithe?"

I told him, and he said, "In that case, I'll lend you a pair of mine. We'll take care of that right now." He stood up. "They'll be a trifle large, I'm afraid; but I'll give you two pairs of thick wool socks. The ladies here knit them, and you'll be glad you've got them tomorrow."

Millie warned us not to miss dessert.

Dr. Fevre had told me that most of the houses here just had ladders to their lofts, although the house where he and our patron were staying had steps, a little crude and pretty clearly homemade but good solid stone steps just the same. Anyway, Dr. Fevre motioned for me to go up the ladder first, and while I was climbing he said, "I would have thrown out those shoes of yours a year ago."

I lifted my shoulders and let them drop. "You know how it is with library resources."

"I do; and I know that they are members of the human race, whatever the law may say. I said I'd loan you a pair of boots. You may keep them, if they fit."

"Then I'll throw out these."

"Good. The boots can pass for shoes if you wear your trouser legs over the tops."

As soon as I saw the boots, I knew that I would never wear them out. They're walrus hide, according to our host on Lichholm, brown but so dark that they generally look as black as an ocean of ink. There are no laces or buckles or anything like that. The tops come up halfway to my knees.

Millie was gone when we got back downstairs. I wanted to know what had happened to her, and Rose told me she was in the kitchen whipping cream.

I said I wanted to show her my new boots and went back there. She had some hand-cranked gadget I had never seen before and was whipping with a will. "Ern, you're a gift from God."

"I know," I said, "but I didn't know you knew."

"Finish whipping for me. It's getting thicker, but my arm's about to fall off."

So I took the gadget and turned the crank a couple of times to see how it worked. Our little bent hostess was nowhere in sight. "I've been itching to get you alone," I told Millie. "I've got a question to ask, and I want you to think before you answer it. When you left the library, you went through the lobby with Rose and the doctor. I was sitting in there, and I saw you."

"Yes, he'd gotten the library to borrow us from Spice Grove, then checked us both out when we got there. I don't suppose you know who got the library to get you?"

"I can guess pretty easily—his wife. Did Dr. Fevre ever check you out of Spice Grove?"

Millie nodded. "Three times. Twice for Rose. You're looking pleased."

"I am pleased. I used to wonder why all three of us were sent here, and all from the Spice Grove Public Library. Now I know."

"If you tell me that'll make two of us."

"All right. You and Rose are easy. He wanted the copies he'd checked out before. A different copy of Millie Baumgartner might have refused to cook for him. He knew you wouldn't."

Millie's nod was slower this time. "And a new Rose Romain might not sleep with him."

"Exactly. Also a new Rose would have to be briefed all over again about what he wanted her to do and how he wanted her to do it. That's probably pretty simple, but it might be complicated. I don't know." I paused. "Want to hear more?"

"Of course I do. What is it, and what's your question? You still haven't asked it."

"I know. The more is that he thought Peggy Pepper was on our boat, which was bound to be difficult. Adah will be difficult, too; but not as difficult as Peggy—or so I think. My question is, could Dr. Fevre have slashed the old Ern A. Smithe's throat with a scalpel as you and Rose walked past?"

Millie stared. "You must be having nightmares."

"It could be done," I insisted, "if he were very quick. Cut the old me's throat and drop the scalpel. I think I saw the scalpel when they cleaned up."

"No. Absolutely not."

I cranked the mixer hard. "If you'd gotten ahead of him momentarily?"

Millie shook her head. "That didn't happen. Rose walked beside him, arm in arm. I walked behind them both. I would've seen it." She paused. "Do you know how the old you lost his arm?"

"I think I do. I think Adah Fevre cut it off."

"Really?"

"Yes, really. She's up and down. Do you know about that?"

"He's talked about it."

"When she's up she goes around with a butcher knife in her belt. I think she got angry with the old Ern, hacked his arm, and sent him back. No doubt the library got a doctor for him, but the arm couldn't be saved."

"Or she cut it off entirely and threw it away. Now whip that cream."

I whipped. "Talking about all this brings me to why Adah wanted an Ern A. Smithe from Spice Grove, and not the Continental Library or someplace else."

"Because you might have talked with Rose and me?" Millie was eyeing the cream.

"Nice try, but I've got a better one." I whipped away. "Because I might have been checked out by faculty members and heard faculty gossip about her husband. Also there was a chance that I might have been checked out by her husband, and be willing to talk about it."

"That's whipped enough." Millie straightened up.

"Does she know about Rose?"

"Possibly, but I doubt it."

"Are you going to fill me in on that faculty gossip? Just what would they be gossiping about?" Millie had been cutting cake; she stopped now, the cake knife raised. "What or who?"

"Not now. Later, maybe."

"That's not fair!"

"Perhaps not, but it's prudent." Three generous slices of cake already lay on three small plates; I said, "What do you say I spoon some of this whipped cream onto those and carry them in?"

Millie nodded and went back to cutting. "Good idea. I'll bring in the rest."

I carried in three pieces, serving Dr. Fevre, our host, and

Rose. By the time I had reclaimed my seat, Millie was bringing in four more for the old woman, Audrey, me, and herself.

Dr. Fevre yawned as soon as we had finished our cake, and Audrey and I excused ourselves. I found that new boots and two pairs of wool socks improved the cold, the snow, and even the dark, starry night enormously. Perhaps it was the wine that had improved Audrey; when we had passed the first few dark houses, she began to sing: "Silent night, holy night, all is calm, all is bright . . ." She knew all the ancient, authentic words, which was ten times more than I did; but I hummed along whenever she lost me.

When she had finished, I said, "You're rushing it. It must be almost a quarter year away."

"Everybody rushes it, remember? Lights and sweaters and everything before Halloween."

"Trees and mistletoe . . ." I was remembering.

"Time to start addressing cards. The last time, I was on that damned island and couldn't have sent any."

I said, "Or gotten any, either. I'll bet your mailbox was jammed when you got back."

"I didn't get back, Ern. I drowned. I told you about that."

I think we were both quiet for a few houses after that, then Audrey said, "Tomorrow we'll be looking at dozens of bodies. Some Christmas!"

"Halloween," I told her.

"They don't celebrate that anymore. Or Thanksgiving or Christmas. Only New Year's. Everyone's supposed to get drunk."

"Give it a thousand years, and maybe they'll discover Christmas again. Look at the Olympic Games. Those were gone for more than a thousand years."

"Do you daydream, Ern?"

I nodded. "Of course I do. Everyone does."

"Me too. Sometimes sailing keeps you so busy you wish you had two heads and six arms; but sometimes the wind is fair and the sails are exactly right, and you can just lash the wheel and skim over the water."

I nodded again.

"I used to daydream for hours then. Someday I'd get married. Maybe I'd have children." Audrey was quiet for a dozen steps. "My husband wouldn't have to be handsome; but he'd be steady and practical, and smoke a pipe. Not a lot, just once or twice in the evening. You know what I daydream now?"

"No, but I'd like to."

"That somebody buys me and gives me as a present."

I never would have guessed that one, and I said so.

"They'd have a birthday party for somebody who loved books and sailing, and there I'd be in a gorgeous gown—or else in sailing clothes. Maybe I'd be carrying one of my books, too. That changes, depending."

"I'll bet the title changes, too."

"You're right. Mostly it's *A Woman Sails Alone*. But it can be other things, too."

I nodded, trying to picture it.

"Sometimes it's a book I wanted to write, but never even got to start. Anyway, everybody would sing 'Happy Birthday,' and then the one who had paid for me would take my hand and lead me over to my new owner. Sometimes that's a woman, but sometimes it's a man."

I said, "I'm glad to hear that," which was the simple truth.

"If it's a man, he has a lovely groundcar, not huge but

luxurious; only when it's a woman, it's usually a bicycle built for two. She sits in front and pedals and steers, and I sit behind her and pedal too. Together we skim along like the wind." Audrey laughed, happy but a little embarrassed. "We weave through traffic. Sometimes she has a penthouse, but usually she lives on her boat."

Maybe we said more than that before we got to the house where they were putting us up, but I have forgotten it if we did. For a minute or two I worried that the door would be locked. Later I found out that nobody on the island locked doors, and your neighbors would be mad at you if you did. They could just walk in anytime they wanted, and you could just walk into their houses. Probably hardly anybody did that late at night, and if you could tell they were busy in bed you snuck back out. I do not know, but I think that's probably the way it is. If I ever walked into anybody's house except that one, I've forgotten it.

There was a candle there in a candlestick, or whatever you call those things. They are like a saucer, only there is a handle like a teacup's and a socket for the candle; on that island, everybody used them. One time I asked about candle making just to make conversation. There is a kind of wax you got from pressing seeds. The rest of the seed was seedcake; you fed that to horses or pigs. Then you mixed the wax with a little seal fat to make it burn brighter. Tie a pebble on a string and keep dipping it into the hot wax until the wax was as thick as two fingers. Cut the string at the bottom and the top, leaving enough at the top to light, and there's your candle.

Which is probably a lot more than you wanted to know. Anyway, Audrey lit our candle in what was left of the fire, then we went up to bed, her first and carrying the candle. I had not figured her as somebody who could climb a ladder carrying a candle, but she did fine. When I got up into the loft, she passed the candle to me. I wanted to blow it out when she started undressing, I do not know why, because I had seen her on the boat. She said I could look as long as I didn't say anything. I told her anything I said would be complimentary, and she told me just keep my mouth shut.

Which I did. The boys had slept together, the old couple had said, and the girls had separate beds. It seemed to me the boys got the best deal, at least in cold weather. I do not think it can be cold all the time on Lichholm, but any warm weather must come really slowly at midsummer and disappear before you have time to hang up your coat.

After five or ten minutes Audrey wanted to know if I was sleepy.

I said, "That depends."

"I'm sleepy. That's what I wanted to say. I ate too much and drank too much. So I'm going to lie down, and if you want to do anything you can do it; but don't expect me to talk or wiggle around to keep you entertained, and if I'm asleep try not to wake me up."

That was fine with me.

10

THE COTTAGE IN THE CAVERN

Next morning I supposed that Audrey and I would hike across the village to the house where Dr. Fevre was staying with Rose and Millie, but we didn't have to. I had just finished shaving when Audrey yelled for me to get my coat on. I did, still wishing I had a warm cap, and tramped out the front door in my new boots and just about all the clothes I had.

I'd seen the sleigh before I stepped out the door, but I hadn't realized that it had come for us. It was pretty big and there were no regular seats for passengers, but there were four bales of straw in back. I sat on one of those.

Audrey sat up front beside the driver. That was going over to the house where Dr. Fevre was staying, and it ticked me off. When Dr. Fevre got in, he sat up front and Audrey in back with me, which I liked a hell of a lot better.

I could smell the food as soon as we went inside to get him, "we" meaning Audrey, the driver, and me. Millie was working her magic in the kitchen: thick bacon and thin bacon, two kinds of sausages, and griddle cakes with lovely dark butter and honey.

Audrey wanted to know how cold it was in the ice caves. Dr. Fevre said it was colder than outside; but there was no wind, so it seemed warmer. Tricky cold, in other words. Maybe that made Audrey feel better, but I decided I could take it or leave it. From what they said, I caught on that Millie and Rose would be staying right here in the village; and to tell the truth, I was tempted to say I'd stay there too and keep them company.

When we left in the sleigh, four bales were barely enough. Dr. Fevre rode up front beside the driver like Audrey had, and Audrey, our patron, Chandra, and I sat on the hay bales in back. After the first mile or two, Adah laid her head on Audrey's shoulder and went to sleep. I smiled, and Chandra whispered, "She was going to stay where we were and go back to bed. Only then she said it would be too cold with nobody to tend the fire or sleep with her."

I said, "Audrey and I took care of the fire. I suppose she's forgotten."

Chandra nodded.

Audrey said softly, "If I keep my voice down, is it going to wake her up?"

I shook my head and kept my own voice low. "I doubt it."

"You look pleased." It was a whisper, but Audrey grinned as she said it.

"I feel pleased," I told her. "Chandra and her mother had separate problems when her mother checked me out, and I said I'd work on both of them. I'll take care of Chandra's as soon as we get back to Polly's Cove. Her mother's was a hand-drawn map she had found tipped into one of the doctor's books. She wanted to know what the island was, and what the square thing in the middle was." I took a deep breath, recalling what had happened when I had touched that square, and shivered.

"Now I think we know the name of the island," I said, "and I believe we're trotting straight toward the square on the map. Dr. Fevre"—I waved at his back—"must have drawn the map soon after he discovered this place. He'd turned up something important here, a thing that the local people didn't like to talk about, and he wanted to make sure he could find it again anytime he came back."

"People here want to keep the ice caves secret?" Audrey sounded doubtful.

"Wouldn't you, if your parents and grandparents, and maybe a child or two, were lying on the ice in there? The first boy you ever kissed, and the little girl you played with when you were her age? Would you want a bunch of tourists swarming around, touching their bodies, leaving candy wrappers and cigar butts in the cave, and taking pictures? I wouldn't."

"They've been pretty open about it while we've been here." Audrey sounded more doubtful.

"You and I are Dr. Fevre's guests. Clearly we know about the ice caves already." When she kept quiet, I added, "Besides, it looks as if he's won their confidence."

"He doctors the sick people here," Chandra told me. "Just because he teaches anatomy people think he isn't a real doctor, but he is. He writes prescriptions and does surgery."

I nodded. "No doubt he does."

Chandra had more to say. "Like, if somebody's got a broken arm or something. He has a place in town. A clinic, like. They just call it the doctor's office, but he brought a full-body scanner. Lots of stuff."

"Good for him."

"He doesn't charge anybody, either. As long as there's something really wrong with them, it's free, like at home. Only fakers have to pay. He told me."

Adah stirred at the sound of her daughter's voice, and Audrey's gesture warned Chandra to be quiet.

There was not much said after that. Mainly, I stewed over the old Ern A. Smithe, his cut throat, and the scalpel I was sure I had seen when the 'bots were cleaning up. I had been just about certain Dr. Fevre had done that, and now he looked worse and worse for it. So who? When? And why? Who else might have a scalpel?

I hope that I have already made it clear that the whole interior of the island was pretty much one big mountain. If I have not, well, it was. There were steep ravines and some side crags and various other details, but basically the ground sloped up and up. The top was snowcapped, like people talk about; but heck, when we were there everything on the island was covered with snow. So that mountain had snow pants on, too, down below its snow shirt.

Being covered with snow pretty much included us; we had been sitting in an open sleigh for almost two hours. When the doctor got down, we got down too and sort of brushed each other off. The sleigh turned around with a silvery jingle of bells, and the whip stirred the horses into a trot. Dr. Fevre started up what might have been a path if it had not been covered with new snow. I followed him, and pretty soon saw a black hole in the snowy side of a cliff, a hole big enough to take both horses and the sleigh. When I saw that, I thought I was looking at the square on the map. I told myself it was a shame we had no shining rectangle here—and then that we might have one after all, a light deep inside that twinkled and seemed to move. After a minute or two, I caught on that what I was seeing was a reflection of our pale sunshine in the ice. Hey, our sun, Sol, is an ordinary yellow-white star, right?

"Careful here," Dr. Fevre called over his shoulder. "There's ice underneath this snow."

There was, but my new boots handled it pretty well. Audrey was used to decks that danced under her feet and could probably have walked up a wall, but Chandra and her mother held on to each other and fell down into the snow twice. I would have helped them up if they had accepted my help. They didn't.

That snow ended two or three steps into the cave. There was nothing but bare ice underfoot from there on in. The cave floor was nearly level though, and we got up onto that as soon as we could. It was ice, too, but the ice was dark and gritty with dirt that had been tracked in over the years. Village people—I could picture them—carrying in their dead on stretchers made of old spars and sailcloth.

I asked Dr. Fevre when we would see bodies, and he pointed back toward the entrance. "You'll see them as soon as the sunlight's gone, more bodies than you'll like."

For a minute it seemed to me that we could not possibly see them without daylight. Then it soaked through to me that there had to be some kind of lighting in there, or else that he had some.

It was the second one. When it was almost too dark for me to see him, he reached into a coat pocket and pulled out light sticks. I had heard of those, but I had never seen them before. You activate them and they put out plenty of light, a kind of pale white light that bleeds out colors. All light in every direction. No heat. Pretty cool, right?

Yeah, sure. Only before long I would have given my watch for some heat. The doctor had gloves, and so did Adah and Chandra. Not Audrey and not me. It wasn't long before we turned off our light sticks and stuck them—and our hands—into our pockets.

Dr. Fevre cleared his throat. "The bodies nearest the entrance are the oldest. Most of them have suffered a good deal of damage over the years. You will laugh at me if I say they are the most dead, and yet I say it."

Nobody laughed.

"I estimate their age at approximately nine hundred years. Many were originally interred with armor and weapons, or so I believe. Those were pillaged long ago."

Adah Fevre murmured, "What a pity!"

"It is. As we go deeper into the caves, the caves themselves become lovely, and the dead more recent. To touch them without purpose would be discourteous to their descendants, the living islanders. Please do not."

Audrey whispered, "I hadn't planned on it."

I nodded.

Dr. Fevre had started off. Audrey had her light stick out again and going, and it gave more than enough light for the two of us. Adah and Chandra brought up the rear, both with their sticks shining.

Here's one of the things that are hard for me to describe. The cave kept getting bigger and bigger as we went in deeper and deeper, not steadily—there was nothing gradual about it—but by jumps. Think of it as a series of rooms, each bigger than the last, and each with a big open arch leading into the next. Maybe nobody would ever build a thing like that; but freezing cold and seeping water had, and it was impressive and inhuman.

Sheets of hard, clear ice hung from the ceiling in most of the caves, and the ceilings got higher and higher and the ice sheets bigger and bigger. Stalactites of ice hung from the ceilings, some of them way up there and some nearly reaching the pillars right under them on the floor; some of those pillars were towering columns of crystal-clear ice that looked as if they were holding up the ceiling.

All that, and all around us lay or sat or stood the dead. Some lay on couches carved from ice. Others stood in niches cut into the ice. Still others lay flat on the floor, just off the path—or two strides off the path, or fifty strides away from the path. Some lay with open eyes that stared at nothing, but most of them looked as though they were asleep.

So now you have some kind of a feel for what it was like for us to be in there. Listen up, this is important. There were side caves branching off from the caves we were going through. Some of those looked small, but some looked like they might be bigger than the one they branched from. The path got smaller and rougher all the time, and in places it branched off into what Dr. Fevre seemed to think were side caves. In a place like that, the worst thing that could happen to you was to get separated from the one guy who knew his way around. So I should have been really careful to keep that from happening—only it did.

Audrey went to look at one body that was way off to the side.

It looked a lot like her, and she thought it might be an early copy.

"Have you noticed her profile, Ern? Most people don't know what their own profile looks like, but I know how mine looks, and this is it. The exact same profile."

I admitted it was close, but I pointed out that the corpse's hair was lighter colored. Audrey's was auburn; this was a pale red.

"It could have faded in here after death. Hair doesn't stay the same when you're dead. It loses color."

I said, "How the hell do you know that?"

She started talking about some primitives she had run into once who shrunk the heads of their enemies and tied them to their belts by the hair. Like anyone would, I pointed out that the color of that hair did not mean a thing. For one thing, it might have been bleached by the shrinking process. And so on.

Audrey interrupted, "How did she die, anyway? She looks as healthy as I am."

Knowing what Audrey herself was like, I said, "By violence, I imagine."

"I don't see any sign of that. No wounds, no neck bruises or anything. You're way too used to assuming that every death is a murder."

"No, I'm not. It's just that I know that the people who prepared her to go in here would have fixed anything like that. Take off that wimple and you might find she'd been stabbed through the heart, or—"

Something touched my elbow, and I turned and stared.

Audrey was already staring. A tall man with washed-out gray eyes was standing there with a flat green box that he held like a tray, silent and expressionless. He had come out of the dark without making a sound. That hit me hard, and a minute later something else hit me quite a bit harder.

There was no one in sight save Audrey and this newcomer. The three of us stood in the circle of light from Audrey's light stick. That lit up a quarter, maybe, of the cavern. The rest was blackness. No doctor, no patron, no Chandra. No one but Audrey and me, and this tall, silent man with his small, flat box.

"We've gotta go!" I was pulling Audrey's arm.

"Which way did they go, Ern?"

The tall man pushed his flat, not quite square, metal box into my hands. At first I didn't want to take it, but he pushed harder. Then I tried to turn it on edge so I could carry it under my arm.

Big mistake.

Everything started to change. Audrey disappeared. The ice pillars were almost trees, and there were small dark things swarming over the roof of the cave. I put the box level again and Audrey was back. She stared at me and rubbed her eyes.

The tall man had started off. He walked slowly, but he took long steps. I said, "Maybe he knows," and started after him, holding his box the way he had.

Audrey said, "The air in here must be bad. I feel sort of dizzy."

"Maybe he's going outside."

"I hope so!" Audrey took my arm then, and it was quite a while before she let go. I was carrying the metal box or whatever it was flat, like a little tray. It was just heavy enough to be inconvenient.

After I don't know how long, ten minutes or half an hour, I said, "See anything you recognize?"

Instead of answering, Audrey pointed. Away off, a tiny beam of white light was darting here and there. I nodded and told Audrey, "That's a flashlight. It's got to be."

She nodded agreement.

The tall man seemed to be walking toward it, which was fine with me. I would have gone toward it whether he had been going there or not.

Audrey called, "Hello! Hello there!"

Somebody answered, very faint. I couldn't make out the words, and I wanted to get out my own light stick and turn it on. No dice on that if I wanted to keep the box flat.

The flashlight beam found us; and Audrey and I shouted. Pretty soon we were near enough to see, dimly, the girl who held it—black curls and lots of them, quilted black jacket, close-fitting black trousers, and high-topped black boots. Pale, oval face. Full red lips and big dark eyes. As we got nearer, I realized there was something familiar about that face. I'd like to prove how smart I am right here, but it would be a lie. I never made her until she told us who she was.

"I'm Peggy Pepper." She had a good smile. "I'm in here looking for Dr. Fevre. Have you seen him?"

"Not lately," Audrey told her, "but we'd like to."

Peggy Pepper turned her light on the tall man. "Do you know where Dr. Fevre is?"

"Sven," the tall man said. It was the first time I had heard him speak, and I got the impression that just that one word had cost him a lot.

"We came in here with Dr. Fevre," Audrey explained, "but we got separated. We'd like to find him or find our way out of here. Either one."

"I can take you out," Peggy said, "and I will after I find Dr. Fevre. That comes first." She paused, and then . . . "You're reclones, all three of you."

Audrey nodded, and I said, "Guilty. I'm Ern A. Smithe, by the way."

"From a library?"

Audrey nodded again. "Audrey Hopkins, Polly's Cove Public Library."

I said, "Spice Grove Public Library, on interlibrary loan to Polly's Cove."

"You screened me once, looking for Dr. Fevre."

I nodded.

"Did he bring you here? All of you?"

I said, "He brought Audrey and me. We don't know where Sven came from, we ran into him right here in the cave. He doesn't talk a lot and he certainly wasn't in the sleigh that brought us here."

Audrey added, "Neither were you. How did you get here?"

Peggy smiled. "I'm supposed to ask the questions, but Hell's bells, why not? The stable in Maiborg rented me a horse. He isn't much of a saddle horse, but he's docile and sturdy. How about you?"

Audrey said, "In a sled. Dr. Fevre got it, but I don't know where."

"A sled? With dogs?"

I said, "Horses. Two horses. I imagine it's supposed to come back later and pick us up. Maybe Dr. Fevre has some way to call it, eephone or something. I don't know."

"I see." Peggy switched off her flash and turned back to Audrey.

"Are you an ancient author, too? How many books did you write?"

"Sixteen."

"Wow! Give me some titles. I may have read you."

"*One Woman Sails Alone Around the World.*" Audrey paused. "*Lost at Sea, Teaching Girls to Sail, Among the Pirates of the Horn, Junks Weren't, My Sheets Are Rigging, Coral Reefs Can Thrill You, You and Your Daughter Can Build a Boat, Safe Anchorage . . .*" Audrey paused to wait for some comment.

"I'm writing a book myself," Peggy said. "My first. Or at least I hope there'll be others after it."

I was tired of carrying the green box by then, so I put it down. "What's the title?"

"*An Atlas of Female Anatomy.* That's just a working title, of course. It's not just the internal organs, it will cover everything. Musculature, skin and eyes, the works."

Audrey said, "Aren't a lot of things the same for men and women?"

"Ah!" Peggy looked pleased. "That's it. At what points are men and women the same and where do they differ? All the standard works deal largely with male anatomy, then some of them consider the exception."

I said, "I suppose that's natural."

"Not really. There are more women on this planet than men, and as far as anybody can tell there always have been. What about you, Smithe? How many books?"

"Somewhere between thirty and forty; it depends on how you count. *The Ice-Blue Kiss, Men Mice and Murderers, Murder for Prophet, Murder's Good for Business, Kill Mama Kill Papa,*

Death on a Daybed, The Corpse Drank Wine, When Will Murder End? Murder on Mars. Is that enough? I always stop there, but I'll name the rest if you want them."

Peggy nodded. "You must have found writing books pretty easy."

"It is if you know what you want to say. If you have to make it up as you go along, you go slowly. Think of it as a wagon."

There was a silence. Finally Peggy said, "I don't understand that at all."

"If your wagon's all built and in good shape, you hitch up the horses and off you go. You should do forty or fifty kilometers a day, depending. If you have to build and rebuild your wagon on the road, you'll be lucky to average ten kilometers a day."

Audrey said, "We should be looking for Dr. Fevre."

"I agree." I picked up the green box and started off in a new direction, realizing after a minute or two that I was following Sven.

Audrey said, "Do you think it's that way?"

I nodded. "Dr. Fevre's not in the direction we came from, or in the direction Peggy came from. Besides, Sven was headed this way. He may know something."

"If he does know, he'll never tell us."

I nodded again. "Maybe he'll show us, and that's better."

Behind Audrey, Peggy said, "You haven't asked me why I want to see him."

I looked back at her. "None of my business. Do you want to tell me?"

"It's the cadavers. I'm taking his classes while he's on sabbatical."

Audrey said, "That can't be much fun, and I imagine you have a great deal to do."

"It is fun, really. I enjoy teaching. The students are horrified for the most part. I can handle a cadaver as if it were an allsweeper, or—"

Audrey said, "There are thousands of them here, and the closer they are the more they bother me."

Peggy completed her thought. "Or a chicken. What's the difference between a human being and an animal?"

"Intelligence, I suppose." Audrey looked at me for guidance. "We're smarter. Wouldn't you agree?"

I nodded. "As long as we're writing the tests."

Peggy said, "You then, Mr. Smithe. What would you say the difference is?"

"We're us. We bury our dead, and sometimes we even bury our pets. There are pet cemeteries. Animals—"

Audrey interrupted me. "Except that we burn them sometimes. My parents were cremated, both of them. That was the way they had wanted it."

I could not indicate the hundreds of frozen corpses with a single gesture, but I got about half of them. "Not always."

"Three hundred years ago people would have said human beings had an immortal soul that fled the body after death," Peggy told us. "I believe that now. Does that surprise you?"

I was looking at the wide cavern we had entered, and I didn't know what to say anyhow.

Audrey said, "That's what your folks thought, I'll bet."

"No, they didn't. They would have laughed at the idea. I've cut up a great many cadavers. Close to a hundred, I suppose. Believe me, the thing that made them human has gone."

I was looking around the ice cavern. "We've never been in this one before."

That sent Peggy's flashlight exploring; its beam was lost in the immensity.

"My goodness, but it's huge!" That was Audrey.

"It is huge, and there's a sort of scree of broken ice ahead." I held up my light stick so the two women could see what I had seen. "It will be hard to get down that slope without falling, and it may be impossible to climb back up. Do we want to go down it?"

Peggy said yes and Audrey no.

"Then here's what we'll do. I'll go down. If I fall, you'll see me. Don't go after me. Tell Dr. Fevre when you find him. He may be able to help me if I'm still alive down at the bottom."

Audrey said, "I wish you wouldn't, Ern."

"Let's assume I get down safely. If I do, I'll try to get back up. If I can't, you two had better turn back." I handed my box to Audrey. "I'll go looking for a way out. As big as this cave is, there may be a dozen."

Maybe I ought to have waited to hear what they would say, but I didn't. I just stuck my light stick in an arm pocket that seemed to have been meant for pens or pencils, walked forward, and started down. The truth is that I was afraid I'd lose my nerve if I didn't. The caves and the cold had been draining away my guts—at least, that's what it felt like.

My guess is that the scree was pieces broken from a really huge ice curtain that fell; anyway, it was made up of jagged flat plates about twice as thick as my thumb. Some were almost as small as coarse gravel, some were as big as a tabletop. Most were somewhere in between. Climbing down would not have been hard if they had been stuck together, and some were. Most were loose. Hard ice—and everything in those caves was frozen hard—is not as slick as ice near the melting point. Water lubes ice, and soft ice melts a little under your weight. The slight friction of this hard ice let me keep my feet, but I nearly fell a dozen times.

Keeping my balance meant waving my arms a lot, and there were two or three places where I had to turn around and crawl down, holding on wherever I could. My fingers were always cold in those ice caves, and they got so cold when I was scrambling down the scree that I had to stop to warm them in my pockets. The cold made my hands weak, too, so weak that I lost my grip a couple of times and started sliding. The scree was long but not very steep—a little steeper and I might have died. By the time I got to the bottom I knew two things for sure.

The first was that I could climb back up if I wanted to, but it was going to be harder than climbing down.

And the second was that I didn't want to.

I had not gone more than a hundred steps or so when I came to another scree. It was steeper than the first one, but a lot shorter, too. I figured I would not have much trouble with it going down or getting up, so I started climbing down pretty confidently. That was when disaster struck.

My light stick fell out of my arm pocket, started rolling and bouncing down the scree, and went out.

I don't know how long I scrambled around in the dark, groping that ice. It was probably only ten minutes or so, but it felt like an hour. Finally I sat down to rest for a minute, halfway determined to start back up blind when I was through resting. I knew which way I had come, or thought I did; and I felt sure I would see Audrey's light, or Peggy's flashlight beam, a long time before I found them.

Then somebody was shaking my shoulder. I opened my eyes, and the light was close to blinding.

"Well, I found you anyway," Chandra said. "I think I'd rather find you than her."

"I'm overjoyed to be found by you," I told her, "and with your light stick we ought to be able to find mine pretty easily."

"Where is it?" Chandra was being careful, holding on with both hands; her light stick hung around her neck.

"Right here somewhere." I had begun looking already. "I had it in a pocket, but it fell out."

"If it went out, it's probably broken."

"Do they break that easily?" I was still looking.

"Sometimes."

"Then it may not be." I was dead set on looking.

"Where's the lady?" Chandra paused. "Audrey. The one you sleep next to. Where's Audrey?"

I pointed up the scree and saw my light stick at once. A short scramble got me close enough to grab it.

"Is it busted?"

I twisted it and it lit up beautifully.

Chandra hesitated. "I'll tell my father she's up there."

"So will I," I said.

We both did, but I am getting ahead of myself. At the far end of that huge ice cavern was something that seemed so completely out of place that I thought I was seeing things. It was a house.

11

Jingle Bells

No, not a cute little cottage with a smoking chimney and some kind of climbing rose blooming pink and white on the front wall; but a house just the same. It was about twenty paces wide, and exactly half as high as it was wide. Maybe it was fifty or sixty paces long, maybe a couple of hundred. I never did find that out.

It was built of blocks of ice. Big square blocks formed the front wall, and trapezoidal ones a nice round arch over that. They fitted so closely you couldn't always see where one ended and the next began.

Chandra had stopped for a minute to let me look. When I had checked out the construction, she said, "This is one of my father's labs. He's got a generator in there and everything."

I nodded to show I understood. I was still too stunned to talk. Then Chandra opened the door, and it was warm inside. Warm and bright. Angels would not—the angels (I'll tell you about them in a minute) did not—have surprised me more.

Adah Fevre was inside, sitting on a little folding chair that had her fur coat draped back over it. Sven was standing behind her, stiff and erect as ever.

Farther back in that long room Dr. Fevre stood between the angels, two radiant blondes. He had turned his light stick off, or maybe just put it back in his pocket, because the light came from ceiling fixtures. I got the feeling that Adah had been talking a blue streak when the door opened and had shut up right away. I'm not sure of that, but that's how it felt. She was leaning forward on the edge of her chair, looking like she was about to spring out and kill somebody; definitely at the top of her cycle. It seemed like she might lose control any minute.

There are times to let other people talk, and times to step up and take charge if you can. This was one of the take-charge-if-you-can kind. I took a deep breath. "You two strolled off and left Audrey and me lost in this God forsaken maze of ice caves. I say you two because I'm not blaming Chandra—she's just a kid. But you"—I leveled my finger at Dr. Fevre—"were the guy who knew his way around, the guy Audrey and I were counting on to guide us."

I paused to give them a chance, but nobody spoke.

"You were the guy who bought us coats and gave me a pair of his old boots, but never got either one of us a hat or gloves. If you want your coat back, I'll fight you for it. If I win, I get your hat and your gloves. I'll give one glove to Audrey."

"You—" Dr. Fevre began.

"I'm not finished yet!" I swung around to Adah. "You're our patron, the fully human lady who had checked out both of us. You walked away from us like you might have set down a couple of magazines because they were too much trouble to carry around. Were you planning to come back for us? We don't belong to you. Do you care about us at all?" One of the angels, a lovely girl of seventeen or so, nodded.

Adah stood up. From somewhere she had gotten a weird hatchet with a straight handle and a spike on the back like a fire axe. "You're correct, Smithe. I left you thinking that the less-than-human I had chosen to solve a point that puzzled me was at least capable of following my husband, my daughter, and me. You failed that simple test. Your library will be better off without you." She raised the hatchet as she finished that, and when she did I got a surprise every bit as big as the warm house of ice or the angels. Sven grabbed her wrist.

"Well done." Dr. Fevre said it absently, like you might pat a dog.

"I could've handled her, but I'm glad you helped." I gave Sven my best smile. "I owe you."

Dr. Fevre told Adah to sit down. It got him exactly nowhere, but he got hold of her hatchet and twisted it out of her hand.

"There are more chairs back there." He pointed toward the dark back of the ice room. "Bring two for us."

I did, thinking it was one for him and one for me, but I was wrong. The blond angels got them both and had to be coached into them. The doctor did the coaching, motioning and touching the backs of their knees to get them to bend their legs and sit. At first their expressions were as blank as Sven's, then one smiled at me. I had known she would have a great smile just by looking at her, and it lit up the room.

"I was explaining to my wife what it is I do here," Dr. Fevre began. "My daughter already knows, or at least knows most of it. Now I'll explain to you as well, and to these two girls."

I interrupted him. "You must know about the screes of broken ice. I left Audrey at the top of one with a brunet called Peggy Pepper. You know her, I think."

He nodded. "She's a coworker."

Adah snorted.

"As a matter of fact, she's taking some of my classes while I'm on sabbatical. That's probably what she wants to see me about."

He turned to Chandra. "Will you be a darling and have a look for those two ladies? You won't be sorry you did, I promise."

I motioned toward the blondes. "Why not send one of them?"

"For one thing, they don't know these caves. Chandra does— rather better than I, I believe. That's enough, but another is that they have no warm clothing. Chandra does, as you know."

I wanted to say she had more than Audrey and I, but that would have brought it down to she's my daughter while you two are reclones. It would not have helped Audrey and me a bit to go there.

"Do you fear that their hearing what I'm going to tell you may cause trouble? It's a reasonable fear, yet you and I must run the risk."

That one threw me.

More softly, Dr. Fevre added, "They need to understand that I chose them when I might have chosen any of a thousand others."

"He has a harem," Adah snapped. "The inmates are dead." She sounded like she was about to walk out; that may have been why Sven was there.

Her husband ignored her. "Most of your experience is a century out of date, Smithe."

"More than that," I told him.

"Yet even in your own time you must have heard or read of

people who had fallen through ice being revived. Their bodies were freezing. Their hearts had stopped and so had all thought. Yet they were restored to life. To normality, or near it."

Looking at the angels, I nodded. They were barefoot, both of them, something I had not noticed before. Something about their long white skirts reminded me that people cover bodies with sheets sometimes.

"Their breasts are lovely," Dr. Fevre said, "I quite agree—yet you might learn several things of interest if you listened to me."

I told him I was.

"That such people—patients who had not drawn breath in an hour or more and whose temperatures had fallen to the point at which water turns to ice—could be restored to life was common knowledge for more than a century; yet no one had acted upon it."

When no one spoke he added, "I teach anatomy."

I nodded. "I know that."

"It is not hard to learn, or very difficult to teach provided one has a sufficient supply of cadavers for one's students to work on. Without those . . ." He shrugged. "It simply cannot be taught well. Any bright child could learn the names of the bones and the notoriously mazed muscles of the back. Drill and encouragement. You wrote novels?"

"Yes, mysteries. Whodunits."

"Could you teach a bright student to write those if he could never try his hand at one?"

I said, "I've got it."

"Just so. The hardest part of my job is securing a sufficient supply of cadavers. A friend joked to me about going to Lichholm. I questioned him, and found he had sighted it when he and his wife had gone on a cruise to Norway. He had asked the cruise director about it, and had been told that it was merely a barren island inhabited by a few fishermen."

"True enough!" Adah snapped. "I would never have come here if I hadn't been looking for you. I know you think I'm insane."

"Disturbed, darling."

"While you yourself are sane. Hasn't it struck you, my darling living doctor, that you and I are surrounded by the re-animated dead? That man you're instructing"—Adah pointed to me—"is dead. These beautiful, speechless girls you're itching to toy with—"

"Adah!"

"Are dead. This guard you've set upon me is dead too."

One of the blondes shouted, "I'm not dead!" and burst into tears.

Sometimes I do things that are flat-out crazy, and that was one of the times. When it happens, it's like I am outside myself watching what I do. Up until then I thought my conscious mind was all alone in my skull; when I ran over to the blonde I found out that there is at least one other mind in there, and saying, *Oh never mind!* does not fix one damned single thing. I was crouched down beside her chair before I knew it and had my arms around her. Want to know what she smelled like?

She smelled like ice.

A whole lot more calmly, our patron said, "You'd better do something, Barry; you're about to lose a concubine."

If he heard her, he gave no sign of it. He sort of patted the sobbing girl's head, smoothing her golden hair, and said, "Of course you're not dead, darling. Adah's being vindictive. Neither the law nor I can hold her responsible for her acts."

I said, "She knows you're alive just as well as we do," and after a while the two of us got the girl calmed down. Pretty soon I found out that her name was Ricci, and when I think of Ricci now I always remember how she pulled up the bottom of that long white sheet-turned-skirt and buried her face in it.

Dr. Fevre said, "All this began when one of my grad students came running to me almost too excited to speak. She pulled me over to the cadaver she had been working on. She had opened the chest—that's standard procedure in my class—and swore she had seen the heart beat. I touched it, and it seemed to me that I could feel a faint tremor. There are half a dozen ways to restart a heart, if it can be restarted. I lacked the equipment for most of them, but I tried two. The heart beat twice, then would not beat again. I told the student to come to my office the following afternoon at three."

I nodded. "Did she?"

"Yes, she did. I told her we had stumbled across a fact of great importance, one that we had to pursue. I promised she would be credited in every paper I published. She gave me the same promise, and we shook hands on it."

I said, "Would I get her name right if I tried to guess it?"

"I'm sure you would. She's Professor Margaret Pepper now."

I nodded. "What did you do?"

Dr. Fevre sighed. "For as long as records have been kept, people have been discovering bodies in tombs untouched by decay. I could spend hours describing all the strange beliefs that have been attached to them. Some people have closed the tombs again and prayed. Others have burned the undecayed bodies or driven stakes into their hearts." He paused. "What's going on, Mr. Smithe? Can you solve the mystery?"

"No," I said. "No, I can't." I was sitting on the floor beside Ricci's chair by then, and when I said that her hand tightened on mine.

"What's the difference between a puppy and the sofa it hides behind? We would agree, I'm sure, that the puppy is alive and the sofa is not. But how do we know that? Is it because the puppy moves while the sofa doesn't? A tree is alive, but without a wind the tree moves no more than the sofa."

I shrugged.

"Biology says that living things grow and reproduce. You see the difficulties, I hope."

I took a chance and said it seemed pretty narrow.

"It does not merely seem narrow, it is narrow. A hen lays a fertile egg. Is that egg alive?"

I said no, that it was the chick inside that was alive.

"A good answer. Let us assume that the chick hatches and in time becomes a hen. That hen lays more fertile eggs. Hasn't the egg we began with reproduced?"

I thought that one over. "I don't think so. The hen's reproducing, not the egg. Besides, the egg hasn't grown."

"Nicely reasoned. I suppose you know how viruses reproduce?"

I shook my head.

"They move into living cells and alter the mechanisms of those cells so that they produce viruses. That is, they produce viruses of the same kind, the kind that reprogrammed them. The viruses don't grow larger, only more numerous."

"I've got it. According to the rule, viruses aren't alive, but we know they are."

"Exactly. Let's not dawdle around trying to produce a better rule. I say that those undecayed corpses are alive. I say it, and I have proved it. In some cases, the heart still beats, like the heart of the cadaver Peggy opened. The heart beats very, very slowly. Perhaps one beat in a week. In others, it does not beat at all. It would be entirely reasonable to assume that the difference is of great importance. In point of fact, it is not."

"The frozen people . . ." I let it trail off, not sure what I wanted to say.

"The great majority of them are truly dead, in the sense that they cannot be returned to life." Dr. Fevre hesitated. "At least not by me. Perhaps another, knowing more than I, might do it. Possibly I myself will be that other in ten years, or twenty."

I asked, "How can you tell?"

"Without trying? I can't tell for sure. I look for bodies that show no signs of injury, no knife-thrust now hidden by a new shirt, no damage to the skull, no sign of disease now more or less disguised, no obvious cancers. When I find such a body, I attempt to revive it. More often than not, I fail. Occasionally, I succeed."

I said, "What about old people?"

Dr. Fevre shook his head. "What would be the point? A heart that has failed will soon fail again. These girls? I examined both carefully, and could not discover the cause of death. Clearly then, they were ideal subjects."

"They died, just the same."

"Of course. The freezing point of seawater is lower than the freezing point of freshwater. Did you know that?"

I shook my head.

"It is. Ice floating on the sea is most often the result of rain or snow—freshwater—falling upon seawater not cold enough to freeze. Someone may have thrown these girls into the sea." Dr. Fevre paused. "People say that God is dead, by which they mean that religion is dead in the modern world. Religion, we now discover, is delicate stuff. Superstition is tougher."

"You think they were sacrificed."

He shook his head. "No, I think they may have been. Beautiful girls, virgins of fifteen or sixteen? Many cults might consider such girls ideal sacrifices. Later their friends or relatives may have stumbled upon their bodies washed up on a beach, or found them floating in the freezing sea. They carried them home and interred them decently in an ice cave thirty or twenty or ten years ago."

I whistled. "I was thinking hundreds of years."

"I doubt it. Their breasts would have been covered then."

An hour or so later, Chandra returned with Peggy and Audrey. Audrey, who was pretty well terrified of it, returned the green box (I'll have a lot more about that later) to me; and we left pretty soon after I got that squared around. There were no spare coats for Ricci and Idona, or for Sven either. The angels wrapped themselves in blankets; Sven signed that he was okay the way he was.

Outside it had started to snow again, so we waited in the mouth of the cave until we heard the jingle of sleigh bells. I do not know whether Dr. Fevre had told the driver to come back at a certain time or called him somehow. It was pretty hard imagining that driver with an eephone, but you never can tell.

All this time, I was itching to get out the map and check

to see if the cave mouth was really the rectangle on it, but I did not dare do it with our patron there in the sleigh with us. She did not know I had pulled it out of the book, contrary to orders, and I was still planning to paste it back in the first chance I got.

12

SOMETHING YOU DO ON A BOAT

Maybe I ought to skip over a good many things now, but I am going to give some of them, like the sleigh being pretty crowded going back to the village. I sat on the floor with Ricci on one side of me and Idona on the other. That was to keep me warm, Dr. Fevre said. I hate people who laugh at their own jokes.

Audrey had a nice, comfortable seat—she sat on my lap. This was one of the few times in my life I've enjoyed being uncomfortable. You never know.

Sometimes the four of us talked, and sometimes it was just Audrey whispering to me, or Ricci, or Idona. Audrey mostly whispered catty things about the two blondes. Ricci told me the story of her life, only without much background and way too many *she's* and *he's*, and not enough names. She was a sweet kid, and she had always wanted to go south of the island she was born on. I kept telling her that she was there now and not to be fooled by the snow. She said she knew it was someplace different because she could not hear the sea. (Only when we got nearer the village, we could.) Besides—here she glanced at me and looked away—the people were different. Nicer.

Idona wanted to talk about sex and did. Had I ever done this? Well, how about that? Did I like it? Did the lady like it? Was it true that two girls could do this to each other? How did I know? Had I watched? Well, didn't I think it was all right for people to watch? Why not? And a whole lot more pretty much like that. Animals and dolls and she used to have a dildo made of walrus ivory. Mostly it had been better than the real thing, only it wasn't warm and couldn't kiss her.

Sometimes I told the truth and sometimes I did not, which was more fun. Of course I was storing up facts and notions all the time. Audrey had been good for sex most nights, but that was bound to stop sooner or later. When it did, would Ricci and Idona be around? And willing? Maybe so—and maybe not.

Ricci would be cozy and a lot of fun, but hard to get rid of if I ever wanted to get rid of her. Also she would make every guy who saw her jealous, which might get me in a lot of scrapes. Idona would be hell on wheels. Sometimes that means lots of fun in bed, but she would be hell on wheels twenty-four/seven.

Prof. Peggy Pepper's flitter seated four, so Dr. Fevre, my patron, Chandra, and Prof. Peggy herself flew back in that. How the rest of us slept on the boat going back doesn't really matter, but I am going to give it anyway in case you care. Audrey and I had Cabin One, up toward the bow and slept on the bunks there, just like two fully humans would. Ricci and Idona had Cabin Two, and Millie and Rose Cabin Three. None of which matters much.

The refrigerated bins were full of cadavers, and when I lay awake at night I used to wonder whether any of them were still a little bit alive, and whether those living ones were conscious sometimes or anyway semiconscious. I wanted to open the bins up and have a look, but the boat wouldn't hear of it. Sure, I had chartered it originally, but I'd signed it over to Dr. Fevre and pocketed the refund. So he was the boss now and an old customer and whatever he said went.

Millie and Rose joined me at the rail the first morning when I was standing out there alone. All three of us kept quiet at first, looking at the sea and the sky. After a while Rose and Millie started talking, how beautiful it was and how grim, both at the same time.

So I said, "This is something you do on a boat when you're out of sight of land—or anyway, that's how it's been for me. On land nobody does it."

Rose shook her head. "You've spent both lives in the city, Ern. Farmers do. In the evening when they're tired especially. They lean over on the fence and look up at the sky, the immensity of it and all the sun and rain, all the fog and snow, and all the winds and birds it holds. All the peaceful still days, and wilder storms than city people have ever seen."

I asked whether she had lived on a farm.

"Yes, I did. I—I mean the first me—was a farmer's daughter, just like the girl in a thousand dirty jokes." Rose smiled, a secret, private smile. "I wrote and wrote when my mother thought I was doing my homework."

Millie said, "You were, in a way."

"I suppose. Then after I got out of school, I wrote when my folks were asleep. I wrote five books, and then the next one sold. That was *Across Magic River*. It sold, and I was so proud!

But I didn't tell my folks until I got the advance. Then I showed them. Nobody laughs at a writer with a check."

I wanted to know if they had tried to take her money.

"No, but they told me how to spend it. No matter what they said, I never promised I would. I'd just nod and say I could see where that might be a good idea." Rose laughed. "What I really did was buy a nice new dress that looked romantic and get my hair done, and have my picture taken. The publisher hadn't asked for a picture, but I decided he might next time. He did, and I sent that one."

I said I would like to see it.

"So would I. I haven't seen it. Not this edition of me, I mean. I've looked in the library, looked every place I could think of."

Millie said, "You should hire a detective. I know a good one, and he works cheap."

"You mean Ern."

"What you really need," I told her, "is a librarian."

Rose nodded thoughtfully. "We're going back to that little library in Polly's Cove, aren't we?"

Millie said, "I'm sure you're right."

"It's old," I told Rose, "and small. Small libraries like that one often keep things that larger libraries would throw out."

"Such as my books."

"And mine." I shrugged.

"Oh, they wouldn't dare!" She was being kind, and I knew it and blessed her for it in my thoughts.

Millie said, "It's not much of a life, being a library resource."

Rose shook her head. "Don't let them hear you say that. They'll burn you."

Millie ignored it. "Do you know what part I liked?"

I said, "I can't guess. What was it?"

"Cooking with our hostess in that cozy cottage in the village. That's what Dr. Fevre checked me out for, and of course the library would never have permitted it if they'd known."

Rose said, "Must I tell what he got me for? Really, do either of you want me to?"

I said, "I'm not curious, Rose."

"You mean you know already. He's got Ricci and Idona for that now."

Millie put in, "Plus Peggy, that fully human girl."

"Plus Peggy. Right."

"Which must be why Ricci and Idona are here on the boat with us." Millie looked thoughtful. "He was afraid they'd make a scene."

"Huh!" Rose was disgusted. "He's afraid Idona will stick her knife in him."

Later I remembered that conversation. It was not important, but I couldn't have forgotten it if I had tried.

13

THE CHEAP DETECTIVE

We got back to Polly's Cove almost a week later than Peggy and the Fevre family. Here I would stop writing if only I could pretend my adventure ended here. The rest gets spooky, and the one-armed edition of me—of your humble narrator, Ern A. Smithe—who cut his own throat was bad enough. Ever since I figured out what must have happened, I've known I may kill myself someday. I don't like it, but I know it's the truth. The thing that I will never do is leave a record like this incomplete. If I'm going to tell my story—and I have already told a lot of it—then I damn well ought to stay alive long enough to complete it.

So I'll try. Here goes.

Chandra returned Audrey and me to the Polly's Cove Public Library. We were both overdue, so there were fines to pay, but they were subtracted from the deposit and just shaved the edge.

Did we mind being returned? Audrey did and it showed, so Chandra kindly checked her out again. I was happy to be back on a library shelf. For years I had wanted to have a real adventure, something truly interesting, complicated, and astonishing, during all those quiet days when I had stood untouched and tried to remember the ins and outs of *Shasta the Cougar* or whatever.

All right, my adventures had come and they had been the real thing, but they were over and done with. Now it was time for me to think about them from 360 angles, how things had looked and how they had sounded. The smell of the sea, and the taste of the various things I'd eaten during those wildly shining days. Would I have put all of them in my books if I could? That was something I thought about a lot; you are holding the answer. I've been scribbling away, and I'm trying.

Then Chandra came in and checked me out for the second time. This time the library did not have to screen Adah. Chandra herself paid the deposit. In cash.

When we were out of the library I said, "It's great to see you again."

She nodded, no smile and no words.

"You seem to be serious as all hell."

She nodded again and took a deep breath. "We need you. The rest of them might not agree with me, but if they don't they're wrong."

I thought that one over and said, "Let's start here. You're in the money. Where did you get it?"

"From my father's stash."

"Dr. Fevre's?"

Chandra nodded, her lips clamped shut.

"He gave it to you?"

"It would take me a long time to explain, Mr. Smithe, and that part's not important." Her eyes were bright with tears, and she was starting to sniffle.

I said, "I'm not going to cross-examine you, Chandra. When you're ready to tell me why you want me, and whatever else matters—"

"I hardly knew him!" It was blurted out. "He was my father and I maybe talked to him a couple of times, but he—he . . ."

"He was your father. Are we talking about Dr. Fevre?"

She nodded miserably.

I said, "Now something bad's happened. We don't have to talk about it now."

"I want to! I have to!"

"And I want to get back to the Spice Grove Public Library," I said. "Sometimes we just have to wait."

We had left the Polly's Cove Library by then and were on our way up the hill, headed toward Adah's high white house with the widow's walk. It was colder now than it had been when we were threading our way through the floating ice on that fishing boat, and there had been a northwest wind that would freeze your marrow. Now Chandra had a red wool coat that made her look grown-up, and a red wool cap with a big tassel to remind you that she was just a kid. I had one of those see-through dust jackets the libraries give us if we are checked out in winter and have enough sense to ask for one. There is no warmth to them (and no batteries, you bet) but at least they stop the wind and keep our clothes clean. I still wanted a cap; that winter it seemed to me that I had been wanting a cap all my life. Climbing the hill to Adah's should have warmed me up, at least a little. Possibly it did; if so I didn't notice it.

Chandra was wiping her nose. When she finished she said, "He's dead, Mr. Smithe."

"Your father?"

Miserably, she nodded.

"What happened?"

"Nobody knows. That's why I got you."

I thought about it. "You want me to investigate. I'm to identify the guilty party and tell you. If I can, you want me to assem-
ble enough evidence to get a conviction or a confession."

"Y-yes."

I thought about that, hard. In the first place, as far as I could
see there wasn't one damn thing in it for me. In the second, the
killer was probably her mother; she had sure as hell been the
one who had mutilated that earlier edition of me.

"How long ago did this happen?"

"Last week. Last Friday."

"Is that when it happened, or is it when you found his body?"

Chandra blew her nose twice. "I'm sorry I'm such a baby,
Mr. Smithe."

"Your reaction is perfectly natural. If you acted as though
your father's death meant nothing to you, I'd suspect you seri-
ously. Now I don't."

Dabbing at her tears, she nodded.

"Did you find his body?"

She shook her head.

"Who did?"

"The lady captain."

"Audrey? Is that who you mean?"

A nod. "Captain Hopkins."

"You said this was Friday. At about what time?"

"Just before supper."

So three full days, plus a few hours. I thought about that and all the rest until we got to the house. In a big stiff-looking room I would have called a parlor I asked Chandra, "Did your mother find anything else? Anything besides the body?"

Chandra shook her head. "I don't know."

"I'll have to question her, of course." I was talking mostly to myself. Louder, "Who called the police?"

Chandra thought about that one. After a few seconds had passed she said, "I think it must have been the house. Mother wanted to keep it quiet."

"Is she angry at the house?"

"I think so, but we don't talk about it." Chandra paused. "She went to bed before they came."

I nodded. "Still, they must have seen her and talked to her."

"Yes." Chandra sounded wretched. "They did, some of them. They woke her up and everything."

For half a minute or more, my forefinger drew circles on the brocade arm of my chair. "What's the name of the investigating officer?"

"I don't know." This, plainly, was a relief. "It seems like there's always a new one."

"I'll have to find out about that."

Chandra was silent. I don't believe she spoke again until she had wiped her eyes and blown her nose, a polite little sound like the chug of a toy train; then she said, "He's gone. I guess you'd like to see . . . but he's not here."

I said, "His body's probably in the morgue."

"I don't know about that."

"It's where they store bodies involved in criminal cases, for a few days at least. After that, the body's turned over to the medical examiner for an autopsy." I was recalling the deaths of Colette Coldbrook's father and brother. "That's if the death looks suspicious. If it doesn't, there is no autopsy."

Chandra gulped. "I guess this looks suspicious, right?"

"I assumed it did from what you said about the police. What was the cause of death? The apparent cause, anyway."

"I don't know what you call it." Chandra stopped and pretended to draw a bow.

"Are you saying he was shot with an arrow?"

She stared. "Can you say that? Shot? When it's an arrow?"

I nodded. "That's the oldest meaning, as far as I know."

"Then that's what it was. A big arrow. Right here." She touched her neck.

"A big arrow? How long?"

She held her hands as far apart as she could. It had been as long as she was tall, maybe more.

I said, "That's a spear."

"Well, it has feathers at the end."

"You've still got it?"

Chandra nodded.

"Who was there at the time? Who was in the house?"

"My mother and father, and your friend the lady captain. Mrs. Heuse—"

"Your parents didn't return Audrey to the library?"

"My father said she could probably stay here if she'd go back there with him. I went along too." Chandra sat down on a stiff-looking davenport. "She did, so my father returned her and paid the fine, only he didn't take his deposit back. We left that in and checked her out again."

I said, "I understand."

"The librarian said we wouldn't be able to if another patron were waiting for her. Only there wasn't anybody, so we could."

"And you did. What about the two girls your father brought back?"

"Ricci and Idona? The dead girls? They're still here." Chandra paused. "I guess I have to invite you or you won't sit down, so you're invited. Sit anyplace."

I sat down in a wingback chair covered with old and badly tarnished tinbroc. "Millie and Rose weren't returned to the library. Are they still there, too?"

Chandra nodded.

"That seems to leave us with no fewer than eight suspects—Audrey, your mother, Millie, Rose, Ricci, Idona, Mrs. Heuse, and you." I sighed. Eight suspects, and all female; the big arrow implied that most women could not have drawn that bow. "You didn't do it?"

"Kill my own father? Heck no!"

I sighed again. I had been listening for guilt, but there had not been any. I said, "It happens. All right, that leaves seven. Have you a favorite?"

Chandra turned her head to look at me. "Do I get to think first?"

I nodded. "Certainly, go ahead."

She did, sitting quietly for half a minute or so. Then, "I've got two. Idona and Rose."

"You must know what's coming next. Why them?"

Chandra shrugged.

"When a married woman is murdered, the murderer is usually her husband. Husbands aren't killed by their wives quite as often, but it occurs pretty frequently. So why not Adah?"

"Two reasons. Because I know her and she'd use her big knife. Besides, I'd know about it if she had an arrow."

I said, "Unless she just got it."

"From where?"

I laughed. "Now you've got me. You picked Rose and Idona. Please explain."

Chandra challenged me. "You don't like me saying Rose. Want to tell me why?"

"I will in a minute. Why did you name her?"

"You were the one who said there were only women left."

I had to think about that one. When I had, I said, "You're right. Rose wants an audience, and not a female audience. If she felt your father didn't appreciate her and was standing in the way . . ."

"Bing! Women know how good-looking she is, but mostly we're jealous. Men are hot for her, or anyway she thinks they are. My father'd had her, but he looked her over a lot just the same. You know?"

"Undressing her with his eyes."

"Yeah." Chandra sounded thoughtful. "Sometimes they held hands. I think Rose might, maybe, kill some man who told her to peddle it somewhere else. Or a man who kept all the others away . . ."

Chandra fell silent. It seemed as if she might talk more without being pushed, so I kept my mouth shut. Someone was walking around upstairs in high heels; I listened to her footsteps and tried to guess who it was.

"Do you want to know about Idona, too?"

I nodded.

Chandra drew a deep breath. "She wants to be queen of the

world. Get in her way, and she might kill you. That's just what I think."

"And you'd like to be wrong."

Reluctantly, Chandra nodded.

"Why is that?"

"All right, I'm sure that's wrong, Mr. Smithe. So why would I want you to believe it?"

"I don't. Why are you sure it's wrong?"

"Because none of it makes sense. In the first place, she'd try to get him on her side. It doesn't matter whether she did or not, because she'd keep trying for a couple of weeks anyway. Probably longer."

I nodded. "You said you had a lot of reasons. Give me another."

"All right, why an arrow? If she stabbed him with it, where did she get it? And why not use a kitchen knife? Mrs. Heuse has lots of them, and she could take her pick. If she shot the arrow, she'd have to get rid of the rest of her arrows and the bow."

I was still digesting what Chandra had told me when the door opened for us and we went inside.

With Dr. Fevre dead, I had expected to find a madhouse, or something close to it. It wasn't really that bad. It seemed like all the women helped with the housework, even though some worked quite a bit harder than others. I offered to help and did, mostly by moving furniture Adah wanted to rearrange or that Audrey wanted to sweep under.

The light in the windows dimmed, the house began to turn its own lights on, and there was a dinner, with me sitting next to Audrey—or her next to me, if you want to put it like that. We held hands sometimes, keeping our hands below the table so no one could see them. That night she and I slept next to Chandra's bed. Women always bitch about men falling asleep as soon as the sex is over, and that night I did. We were still holding hands when I dozed off; I don't believe I will ever forget that.

When I woke it was still pitch-dark in our bedroom and something was in the room with us. Ninety-nine times out of a hundred no one will notice a small animal as long as it keeps quiet. My visitor did, only he was not even close to small. He was as quiet as a shadow, moving very, very slowly. That helped a lot, but the floor was not quiet; it creaked and groaned beneath his weight.

Maybe I should have elbowed Audrey until she woke up, but I didn't. She might have screamed and for all I knew screaming might get you killed. Sure, I would have tried to protect her; good luck to that, because whoever he was he was so big he seemed to fill the whole room.

The door opened, and for a second or so I could see the rectangle of faint light. Then the doorway was blacked out by somebody one hell of a lot bigger than I am.

Oh so quietly, the door closed behind him.

I had not realized how frightened I was until I tried to sit up. Then I found out—my whole body was trembling.

It seemed like forever before I could make myself sit up. Maybe I was brave, but my body was scared half to death just the same. Getting out of bed was even harder.

I opened the door as quietly as I could and looked out. Our bedroom had been dark, but there were a couple of little lamps in the hall. Whoever it was that had been in our bedroom was gone.

So was the big arrow somebody had pulled out of the doctor's neck.

Could whoever our visitor had been have climbed out a window? Probably not—he'd been too big. So front door or side door or back door.

I went around to all three. Mrs. Snow bolted them all at night, or so I had been told. I checked them all, and they were all unbolted, the big iron bolts pulled out of their sockets by somebody inside. Maybe he was still inside with us. Maybe he was gone, which I liked one hell of a lot better. I found a lamp in the kitchen and checked out the empty rooms on the second and third floors. Nobody.

Basement? Nobody there, either.

14

OF THE CONTINENTAL POLICE

I've been getting ahead of myself. Let me back up a little and fill you in. The natural thing would have been for Adah to take charge, since it was her house. All right, but she wasn't a good candidate for taking charge of anything. When she was up she was in the same league as Napoleon, sure; but when she was down she couldn't have run a kid's playhouse. So it was Audrey, which gave me another reason Chandra had called her the lady captain. Or maybe I ought to say it was Mrs. Heuse in the kitchen and Audrey in the other rooms, which explains it exactly. Could I have taken charge? Maybe, but I didn't want to be in charge and didn't try.

I quizzed all of them instead, first as a group and then talking to individuals in private. From the group I learned nothing much. Adah felt that somebody or other was trying to take her house away from her and Ricci was certain that the house was haunted. Of course I wanted to know why each of them felt the way they did. Adah just felt like the way she did and kept insisting that it was her house. I agreed with her, but she argued about it with me just the same. You probably know the type.

Ricci had seen a shadow that had her spooked. That shadow had not been anybody's, she said. It was just there for a minute, then it disappeared.

There were a lot of rooms, as I've probably mentioned before, but not enough furniture for all of them. You could have a private room if you were willing to sleep on the floor like Audrey and me. Only we nixed the private room; I slept with Audrey next to Chandra's bed. (You would probably have guessed that if I hadn't told you.) Chandra had called her the lady captain, which made her sound like a woman who ordered other people around. That was maybe a little bit true, only with me it was only once in a while. Audrey and I had a lot in common, and it meant we were on the same team. Every team needs a captain for the coin toss and to talk to reporters; but "captain" doesn't mean much when the team's on the field. I wanted to get back to the Spice Grove Public Library where I belonged. Audrey belonged to the Polly's Cove Public Library, but she didn't want to go back there, or at least not very much. From time to time we tried to figure out a way to get her into Spice Grove with me.

About midnight Chandra started yelling that there was somebody under her bed. I turned over in a hurry and had a look, and there was nobody. So I said he was gone.

Next morning, I got out my notes and read over what each of the women had told me. Nobody had a decent alibi because I could not fix the time closer than a couple of hours. Nobody seemed to be lying, either; but I felt sure that somebody had to be and kept pounding away and getting nowhere. After thinking it all over, I shrugged and sighed, and decided they were telling the truth.

That meant Dr. Fevre had killed himself—or that the killer was somebody from outside who had gotten into the house. I hadn't known him all that well, but he had never seemed like the suicidal type. All right, maybe if he'd been breaking his back on something really big and it had failed. Maybe then. But what was it? I couldn't think of a damned thing, and there had not been a whisper of anything like that in what the girls had told me. From somewhere he'd gotten that big arrow. Ah, the very thing, he had said to himself and stabbed himself in the throat with it.

And snakes ride bicycles.

Plus there was other stuff. Suicides usually leave notes, and the better educated they are the more likely a note is. No note, and Dr. Fevre had taught classes at the university for Pete's sake!

That was not all. Suicides mostly threaten and talk about it for weeks. I screened Peggy Pepper, who had gone back to her apartment, and asked her. She said no, nothing like that.

Then too, there was the big arrow. None of the girls had known he had anything like that, or so they said.

Fine. It had been somebody from outside. Probably he'd used a bow and arrow because they don't make much noise. Also you didn't have to get close; he could have shot through an open window. After that I was stuck, which is the problem with hiring a cheap detective.

We slept in the house that night. Sometime pretty close to sunrise, I woke up. There had been footsteps in the hall outside, I was dead certain. Now somebody had opened the door to our room.

I waited. Audrey was still asleep, snoring softly beside me. Our patron hadn't stirred. Scare them and they'll run, I told myself. I wanted to catch whoever it was (I thought probably Adah or Rose) and explain that as a general thing I murdered midnight visitors. Then he stepped into the moonlight for a minute, and I caught a glimpse—a big guy wearing some kind of helmet with feathers. I had seen feathers on women's hats once or twice, but never on a man. He got close and I grabbed for him and got something that came loose, then he was gone. I must have let go after that; I didn't hear anything hit the floor, but I probably should have.

I found it on the floor in the morning when I got up. It was a big knife, different from anything I'd ever seen. I'll try to fill you in on it without beating it to death.

The big heavy blade was curved a little and sharp on both sides. The guard was a simple flat bar of something that looked to me like copper. The grip was pinkish-red and seemed to be some kind of stone, only not very heavy; it had finger grooves that were too far apart to fit my hand; I had to ignore them when I gripped it. The pommel was copper or something, like the guard. You could see where the tang went clear through and was pounded flat to keep the blade from pulling out.

It all adds up to a really nice knife, and I would have kept it and worn it if there had been a sheath. As it was, I put it away hoping to get somebody to make me one or make one myself. It never hit me that the guy who owned it might come back looking for it.

Like I've said, I was overdue. I told Chandra and her mother about that, and just as I figured Adah told Chandra to take me back and collect the deposit. Sometimes I felt sorry for that kid;

it's not fair to make kids responsible for grown-up stuff. Sometimes you have to, but with Chandra it seemed like it was all the time.

So back to the Polly's Cove Public Library, and a shelf nowhere near as nice as the one in Spice Grove. I took the knife with me and hid it behind some books. Don't bother to look, it's not there anymore.

Audrey and I were not supposed to shelve side by side, but Audrey asked Charlotte to put us like that. It made our Dewey Decimal Numbers wrong, but the librarians didn't seem to notice. We didn't even hold hands until after six, when the library closed.

So swell. Only after a couple of days some fully human guy I had never seen before came in and checked out Audrey. I would have stuck my knife in him if it would have done any good. In a way, I was glad it wouldn't; how would she feel about me if she knew I was a murderer? As far as I had known, the guy had done nothing wrong. Audrey had been a circulating library resource. In two weeks he would have to return her or check her out again. So whistle, whittle, and wait.

About a week later, a tall, hard-faced woman with a brown braid hanging down her back checked me out. She had a groundcar, big and plain ebony. I thought I knew something as soon as I was in the front seat next to her and got a look at the dashboard; so I said, "Polly's Cove, Officer?"

That got me a sidelong glance, very brief. Then, "I'm Continental, Smithe."

This time I actually whistled, without making much noise.

"You're a reference, is that right? Sort of a dictionary with legs?"

I admitted I was, only not a dictionary.

"A historical reference to your own work."

I nodded. "That's right, although I don't actually remember everything."

"What about your life. Are you a reference to that?" Here it came, and I knew it. I nodded again. "My work was my life, more or less."

"You wrote . . . ?"

"Mysteries. *Who Killed Cock Robin?* Clues on pages twenty-six, a hundred and five, and two hundred and ninety-nine."

"A lot of people you've known must have been murdered in that case." She wasn't serious.

I grinned. "Not really. They just should have been."

No laugh, not even a smile. "You knew Dr. Fevre."

"Slightly. I've met him and spoken to him."

She watched her driving, not looking at me. "Did you like him?"

I had to think that over. "I admired him. If I'd gotten to know him better, I might have liked him."

"But you don't think so. Why not?"

"You had to know him."

"Which you did, a little. Why didn't you like him?"

"He's not alive to defend himself. Can't we talk about something else?"

"Not now, Smithe. Why didn't you like him?"

I said, "Suppose you were to show me a forest I'd never seen before." I didn't have to think about it.

For a moment the lady cop turned to look at me. Then she said, "My name's Katrine Turner, Mr. Smithe. Do you want my badge number?"

I said it was a pleasure, and the number wasn't necessary.

"Now tell me about your forest."

"I'd look it over and think about hiking and fishing. Maybe hunting. Sitting under a tree, reading poetry and listening to a brook. Dr. Fevre would look it over and think about lumber."

Katrine was quiet for a few seconds. Then she said, "I never knew a library reference would be so much fun to talk to."

It was a compliment worth filing away for the dark hours. I said, "I never knew a policewoman could be such a charming friend."

"Thanks, you win. Will you help with my investigation? You ought to, after that."

I was tempted to say that since she was fully human and I wasn't I'd have to. It was true, but it would've taken us into territory I didn't want to visit; so I substituted, "All I can, certainly. How can I be of help?"

"You weren't there when Dr. Fevre was killed. Correct?"

I nodded. "Correct. I was sitting on a shelf in that rather unpleasant library."

"Would you have killed him if you could? Honestly now. Lies won't help me."

"No. I would not."

"Why not?"

"For a long list of reasons. How many do you want?"

"What's number one?"

"I'm a reclone. Dr. Fevre was fully human. If the authorities— that's you, among a million others—so much as suspected I had killed him, I'd be burned."

"Let's have more."

"Killing him would be morally wrong. Maybe I should have

led with that one. I have no right to make private judgments or perform private executions. Third, I had nothing to gain by his death. Fourth, he had never harmed me or even insulted me. Is that enough?"

"Not quite."

Polly's Cove was some distance behind us now. Pastures held little fawn dots I decided were dairy cattle. Most of the houses had pointed towers and big featureless buildings that were probably silos and barns. I wondered where we were going, but this seemed like a bad time to ask.

I said, "On top of the reasons I've already given, his daughter, Chandra, had checked me out. She did it as her mother's surrogate, but I felt that she was my patron. The law would say she wasn't, but that was how I felt. Legally I'd be killing my patron's husband. Emotionally I'd be killing my patron's father."

"Go on."

"Dr. Fevre had checked out two of my friends, Millie Baumgartner and Rose Romain. Naturally they were deeply grateful; we always are when anybody checks us out. They would've spoken well of me, just as I speak well of them. Dr. Fevre and I were acquainted, and so on; there seemed to be a pretty good chance that he might check me out someday. We're burned when there isn't any reader demand for us. Do you know about that?"

Continental Turner nodded. "It must be a hell of a way to live."

"You get used to it," I told her.

We were silent after that, while I reflected that a Continental cop was at least as likely to be shot as I was to be burned. That must be a hell of a way to live, too.

15

Strangers in the House

For the first few kilometers, I thought we were on our way to police headquarters in Polly's Cove. When we finally got to where we were going, it turned out to be a cluster of gray buildings surrounded by a high concrete wall. Wide steel gates half opened to let us in, and shut behind us fast and with a solid clang. The silence that followed made me think there might be no prisoners and for that matter no guards. In a room on the top floor of a building without windows I was told to sit in a machine with half a dozen dials and a big screen I couldn't watch. A helmet was positioned on my head and I got quizzed all over again, this time by a little man with rimless glasses. I told him the same things I had already told Katrine Turner. They didn't satisfy him, and after a while I got the feeling that nothing ever would.

It was already pretty dark when I was brought back to Katrine and her ebony groundcar. It had seemed to me that the examination went on forever; it must have been six or seven hours really. "I'm supposed to bring you back to the house where

I picked you up," Katrine told me. "Would you rather go some-place else?"

I said yes, that I'd rather go where I belonged, which was the Spice Grove Public Library.

"I can't go that far, but I'll talk to the people in Polly's Cove about you."

I thanked her. Coming from a Continental cop it was bound to do some good.

"Do you know, I don't think I've ever asked your opinion, Smithe. Who do you think murdered Dr. Fevre?"

"I don't think, I know." I sort of braced myself, feeling pretty sure she wouldn't believe it and I might get slapped around for saying it. Being a library reference can be tough. Trust me, it often is.

"A big guy in a pointed helmet with feathers and gadgets on it," I said. "He came out of a side passage on my floor. I've gone down that a little way and tried to open some of the doors—there must be a dozen of them—but all those I tried were locked." I shut up for a minute, thinking and wondering whether she'd believe me. "I'd never seen the big guy before, and I haven't seen him since. But I know damned well he did it."

When I'd finished, she wanted to know if I'd used tools on the doors, an axe or something like that. I said no. What good would it do? Just make the big guy mad at me, and we knew he'd kill.

"Could you show me the passage?"

I tried to say sure. You know how that came out.

"If the doors won't open, you and I will force one."

Which is pretty much what we did.

Saying it like that makes it sound simple and easy, but it

wasn't. In the first place, I did just about all the work while she supervised. In the second, I had to scare up—or get her to buy—my tools. By the time we had the first door open, I had a pry-bar, a drill, an axe, and some other stuff. The first two I got out of the tool chest on the boat. The rest I had to buy with Katrine's money. When she said she was sorry the door was so tough, I told her that the last door like this I'd seen was steel. This wood was hard and thick and bound with iron straps, but steel would have been a ton worse.

I tried to sound cocky through all this, but really I was worried half-sick. Those steel doors had been put there by one of us, and I was pretty sure I knew who it had been. These doors had been put there by people from the other side.

How did I know that? Simple, everything showed it. Those others had not been much different from the lid of a strongbox or the door of a safe. This one was hardwood and the wood wasn't ponticwood, oak, walnut, or any other wood I knew, wood as hard and heavy as iron and so thick the boards made me think of timbers; its four hinges were two-piece (meaning no separate hinge pins), a design I'd never seen before. The screws that held them had five-sided heads and no slots.

So had Dr. Fevre hired himself a carpenter and had that door put in? No way! Colette Coldbrook's dad had put in those other steel doors; these doors were from the other side. We had gone through those first ones and messed around in somebody else's world; somebody else was coming through these to mess around in ours. I was one of the natives he was studying, or maybe just one of the natives he was less than eager to meet. It was a concept I had a tough time accepting, but I knew it was the truth.

After an hour or so of hard work, Katrine wanted to know whether I was sniffing or just breathing hard. I explained that I was doing both.

"Just what do you mean by that, Ern?" She sounded as though she were really interested.

"Sniffing because the air coming in smells different and good. You want to fill your lungs with it."

She came over and sampled it herself. "Not like sea air," she said.

I agreed.

"Have you ever smelled jungle air, Mr. Smithe?"

"I don't believe I have."

"It smells of leafy green things growing and growing, and rich damp mold that is heaven to plants. This isn't like that." She went quiet.

"Or like the sea, you said."

"Right. This smells empty, or almost empty. Sun and leaves."

I was glad she had pinned it down for me. I said, "Sort of like jungle air, only not warm or wet."

"You said you'd never smelled that."

"I haven't, but I've read about it. I know what it's like, or anyway I think I do."

I had been prying at the boards, and a minute later one of them broke, letting me see in.

It took me a couple of blinks to sort out what I was seeing. The room was round and almost empty; no ceiling, just a funnel-shaped roof with no smoke-hole at the top. After that I tried to figure out the walls: they were dark brown wood with whitish stuff in the vertical cracks between the boards that might have been caulk or plaster or almost anything. No windows, but an open doorway with thick walls and bright sunlight showing through it.

"Are you going out there?" She was pushing past me.

I shook my head. "No way."

"Why not?"

"Somebody doesn't want us to. The door I broke was there to stop us. They won't like it if we go outside."

Katrine was quiet for a minute; then she said, "I'm going and you're coming with me."

"No way!" This time I made it just as solid as I could. "No, I'm not!"

"Yes, you are. Bring that axe."

I told her to go to hell.

"We're going out there, both of us." That was the first time I'd seen her pocket rocket; now I saw it, head-on.

"Each missile carries a pinch of high explosive. It goes off inside you."

I told her I knew that.

"Fine. Go in there or you'll find out how it feels. Bring the axe."

I wanted to tell her she wouldn't do it, but the words never got out of my throat. Her eyes said she'd shoot me as soon as I said she wouldn't, and she was fully human and a Continental cop. Who was going to arrest her for smoking a reclone? Nobody!

I stepped inside, and after I'd caught my breath I went over to a window. Behind me she muttered, "Shakes you up."

I wanted to say it did, every time; but I had sense enough

to swallow it. Besides, just going to that window and looking around gave me a dozen other things to think about.

Over my shoulder Katrine said, "No violent storms here." It was close to a whisper, and I looked back at her.

"High winds would blow down these trees, so no trees or twisted trees no bigger than bushes. That's how it is with us."

I hadn't known that.

"These trees are bigger than . . ."

She had paused; I just waited.

"Do you know where we are, Mr. Smithe?"

"In a useless kind of way, yes."

"Tell me!"

"We're on the Earth-type planet of some other sun. Next you're going to ask me how I know."

"No. I'd ask you why you think so, but I can guess the reasons. That doesn't mean I'm buying the idea."

"Your doubting doesn't change the fact."

Katrine caught up with me. From then on we walked side by side. "I take it you've been here before?"

I shook my head.

"But you know anyway."

"Right." I nodded.

"Well, I don't; but I'll keep it in mind. How do we get home?"

"Just turn around and walk back through the door."

I started to turn, and she caught my arm. "Wait up, Mr. Smithe! The man who murdered Dr. Fevre came from here? Is that what you're telling me?"

"Yes. He did."

"And presumably he came back here, went home."

I saw where that was going and shrugged.

"A big man wearing a pointed cap, you said."

"It wasn't a pointed cap. It was more like a helmet, only with earflaps."

"Right. Now tell me something, else, Mr. Smithe. Why did someone come from here into—into the place where we live and kill Dr. Fevre?"

"Maybe Dr. Fevre came in here first and did something people here didn't like—killed one of them or ticked off the wrong person."

There was more after that, but none of it is worth writing down.

16

Among the Leaves

When she had asked half a dozen more questions and I had explained that I had no idea, we looked out of a window together. Sure, I should've gone down the steps with or without her; but I wanted that missile pistol with me. If she'd have given it to me, I'd have left her behind and walked away whistling. As it was, I felt I'd have to take it from her cold, dead hands. Maybe I could have gotten behind her and choked her, only the consequences of that looked really bad if I stopped before she died, and they could have been even worse if I had killed her. (Not that I was sure I could bring myself to do it.) Should I leave her body here, so the big guy who shot Dr. Fevre would know straight off that I was a murderer too?

Shove it back through the door where somebody from our boat would find it?

We groped and stumbled down the dark wooden stairway that wound down the inside of the hollow tree I still thought of as a building. I kept expecting to run into somebody, but we didn't. When we finally got to a door, I said, "From what I saw up there, this area is full of trees and brush. Are we going to try to find our way through them?"

Katrine didn't bother to look back at me. "There must be somebody here."

"There is," I said. "We are." I wasn't hoping for a laugh, which was a good thing because I didn't get one.

If you've never explored a whole new landscape, you might think there isn't much to see. Really, I think it depends on what interests you.

Suppose you're really interested in sailboats, like Audrey. If you come across a new boat, not exactly like anything you've seen before, it's going to take you an hour or more before you know the ropes—how the standing rigging's set up, and how the halyards are—plus why they're like that, what the crew can do from on deck and what somebody will have to climb here or there to take care of.

All right, an innocent little path on another planet can be ten times worse. This gray-brown one was rounded the way they do roads so the rain will run off to the sides. That was the first thing I noticed. It seemed like there were woods on either side, trees so big their branches met high up over the path, making it shady, although little bright spots here and there showed that the day was sunny way up past the highest leaves. I took in all that right off, maybe ten minutes before I nearly killed Katrine.

Even today I don't like to think about that part. First let me say I never meant to. She started to slip, and I snatched at her and she must have thought I was trying to push her off, because she went for her pistol. I grabbed her hand before she could shoot me and got my finger into the space behind the trigger. That kept her from firing; she couldn't move the trigger back far enough. Twice I came too close to the edge and the round side of the limb almost sent me stumbling off backward. Then she did. I wrenched her arm, catching the barrel with my free hand. She must have let go, because she stumbled back too far—so far she couldn't stop.

It was quiet up there after that, just a soft whisper from the leaves, so I heard her fall even though I never actually heard her hit the ground. Twigs snapped and popped, the noises fading out. Like I said, I didn't hear her hit bottom, and it seemed to me she might be alive, probably badly hurt, somewhere down below.

Before that I hadn't ever handled a launcher pistol, the thing a lot of people call a pocket rocket; but I found the safety in half a minute or less. It looked to me like it was off, so I moved it to hide the bright little stone. After that I sort of aimed it up and tried to pull the trigger. It wouldn't budge.

So I fooled around with it, pushing that safety up and down and got disgusted with myself. Not just disgusted, but good and mad. The next time I didn't bother to aim, just tried to strangle it when I pulled the trigger. There was a whoosh that ended in a thud, then a sound like a blow from a hammer. Another limb, one so far away that it was almost out of sight, trembled and sagged, its heartwood breaking with enough noise that I could hear it grind and snap.

All of a sudden, I was scared.

What if Katrine were dead, lying way down there on the ground? Would I be a murderer? Maybe she was just hurt pretty badly? Could I go off and leave her? She hadn't been a real enemy, just a lady cop trying to do her duty.

By the time I had thought about all that, I was at the trunk and scrambling down the rough bark. It was good about providing footholds and handholds, but pretty often they broke under my weight. That was less fun than it sounds like. I just about fell a dozen times.

Then I was almost down, and I could see Katrine lying on the moss, not close but not so far away that it was hard to spot her.

I started to climb down the rest of the way, finding footholds in the rough bark. I was tired, and about halfway down I stopped to rest and think.

Suppose Dr. Fevre had come here. The way it looked to me, the guy who killed him had come to our world with a mission, had done it, and had gone home as soon as it was over.

So justice, maybe. Or plain old revenge. It could even be that he'd had Dr. Fevre mixed up with somebody else. Until I knew more I had no way of judging. Our door had been in Adah Fevre's house. The big guy's was in some kind of weird wooden temple high up in the biggest tree ever.

That got me wondering about the doors' locations. The steel door up on the top floor of the Coldbrook house made sense because it was close to the pile that powered it. I decided this one might be too, I just hadn't looked in there.

I started looking around for it, and that was when it hit me. All my life I'd lived in two dimensions. Oh, sure, you were on the bottom shelf and somebody else was on top, on the highest shelf; but that was kid stuff. The forest floor I was seeing was more of the same; only when we went down from the library building I could turn around and look back at the place we'd come out of, windows showing you where the floors were, window after window in a long, shining stripe that went clear to the top.

How do you think of Trouble? I usually picture it as a tall, dark somebody walking around behind me and waiting for his chance to screw things up. As I worked my way down the trunk I couldn't get away from the thought that Trouble looked a heck of a lot like me. Most of the trouble I've had in my life I've made myself. I should have gone back through the door right off, and I had known it. Here I was climbing down into trouble freely and on my own. I should have said to heck with her, shut the door behind me, and bolted it as tight as I could.

Only I hadn't. I had seen a good deal of my own world—this is what I told myself. I'd sailed its seas and flown over a lot of it with and without Colette Coldbrook. Now I wanted to spend a day, one day at least, looking over this one. My axe had been getting in my way as I climbed, so when I had settled on a one-day minimum stay I pulled it out of my belt and dropped it.

In my imagination, I asked Katrine how long she was planning to stay. My imaginary Katrine said exactly what I'd been expecting—that she would stay as long as it took to meet up with Dr. Fevre's killer and bring him to justice.

"And you want me to tag along until you do."

Surely you want to see justice done, Mr. Smithe.

I said, "I guess I'm supposed to nod."

Up to you.

"All right. No, I don't."

Then you won't help me?

Here it was. I thought it over before I answered that one. Finally I said, "I'll help you for as long as it makes sense to. If you go on past that, I won't."

By the time I got down to her, she was sitting up, shaking her head and trying to stand. I helped her up and gave her back her pistol.

After that, we walked together, me with my axe and Katrine with her pocket rocket. There was a lot of stuff to see, none of it including people.

The trees were definitely spooky. To get the feel of how it was for us, you have to keep in mind that those trees were as big as big buildings, trees as tall as skyscrapers and different from any trees we've got here, giant trees watching, waiting, and listening. Once I tried to pick some fruit off one, but the fruit rolled around until it could see me, and its pupils were like a cat's. That stopped me cold.

Maybe seeing my axe put their nerves on edge or maybe Katrine's pistol did it. Or they both did. I never did find out. Whatever it was, their roots moved around down under the earth, making it rise in little rippling hills, and the red, beady eyes that grew on some branches kept watching us. Maybe it was just that we were people and could walk around. Trees don't think that's natural, or that's how it seems to me. Whatever it was, we bugged them.

The grass was sort of spooky, too. Sometimes it moved when there was no wind, and sometimes it didn't when there was one. Something else was going on, and I couldn't figure out what it was. There are plants that catch bugs, but there were no bugs where we were for the grass to catch. It moved anyway, and I never did figure out what it was up to.

Right here I guess I ought to lie and make up all kinds of weird stuff I could say happened. Nothing did right then, really. The grass and trees were weird enough all by themselves, and if you've never been in a place like that, where you shiver in spite of a warm wind, there's no use my going on about it.

We camped that night, if you can call it camping when you

haven't got a tent or sleeping bags or even a couple of blankets. Katrine killed a skinny white tree with her pistol, and I chopped it up. When that was done—it seemed like it was all bones—I made a pile of chips and splinters that her pistol set on ablaze. Shoes and boots off, we lay with our feet nearest the fire and our heads as far from the smoke as we could get them. I think she was expecting me to try to rape her and was getting set to kill me when I did. So I didn't. Maybe you won't believe me, but I wouldn't have done it anyhow.

That night I had a dream. I was sitting at a table in Alice's Tea Room. Everything was terribly real except that the floor was glass. I could look right through it and see the traffic way far down below where buses, groundcars, and trucks were moving along a busy street a hundred stories down. It felt awfully real and somewhere the glass was cracking, an incessant, unmistakable sound like fingernails scratching at a whiteboard. Soon the floor would fall and I would fall with it, fall far, far down onto the pavement of the street below.

Next morning we found the man we had come through to arrest; he was standing over us with Katrine's pistol stuck in his belt. When he gestured to tell us to roll over, it was with the short broad-bladed chopper in his right hand. We rolled and he started to tie us, me first.

That was a mistake. As soon as his hands were busy with me and the rope, Katrine jumped him.

He was a lot bigger than she was, and stronger, too. She was faster, and knew exactly what she was doing. I reached into the fight, grabbed her pistol out of his belt, and shot him with it.

After that, I reached out to Katrine, offering my hand to help her stand up. I was surprised when she took it.

For half a minute, maybe, she dusted herself off and adjusted her clothes; then she said, "That does it. We're going back."

I nodded and handed over her pistol, then we went back through the door together. When we'd had something to eat and were drinking kafe, I said, "Maybe I'm wrong about this, but it seems to me I ought to know what you're going to tell your bosses. If they have somebody ask me questions, our stories ought to match."

She grinned. "Because they'll try to beat it out of you if they don't."

"All right, that's part of it. Are we going to tell them about the door?"

She gave me the look. "Do you really think I'm that dumb?"

I shrugged. "I don't know. I guess that's what I'm trying to find out."

"Fair enough. No. If I thought they might send somebody to see if I told the truth, I might. They wouldn't. They'd work on me and have a shrink work on me, and I'd probably end up shuffling papers for the rest of my life."

"What'll you tell them?"

"The truth." She leaned back, enjoying her little rehearsal. "I found Dr. Fevre's murderer, but I could never learn his real name. He resisted arrest, and I was forced to kill him. Case closed."

I said, "If they do send someone I'll back you."

17

SHELF LIFE RESUMED

When we were back in Adah's house, I explained to a couple of the ladies that I was overdue; eventually they nodded. Then I said, "I doubt that anybody will question me, but if they do it would be nice if you would back me up."

After that Chandra and I strolled down the hill to the library. That short walk should have seemed familiar—but it felt terribly, terribly strange. Every step we took was rerunning a part of my life that I remembered much too vividly, running my life backward. I understood that, but my heart snatched at straws. For maybe half a minute, I thought we'd stop for cantaloupe smoothies, but Chandra vetoed that, so we didn't. As we strolled along, she told me what a good idea it had been to check me out, and I explained to her what a bad idea it had been.

When she had returned me and my card had been stamped, she collected the deposit minus the overdue fee and gave me a kiss on the cheek; before I could think of a good way to say good-bye, she had gone.

"She enjoyed you." One of the part-time librarians smiled.

I nodded and decided it would be safe for me to say that she was a good reader, so I did. Then I asked about Rose and Millie.

"That's right, the three of you came together, didn't you?"

I nodded, thinking about our ride in the truck and half a dozen other things.

"What is it?"

"I was just wondering about them. I happen to know that the patron who checked them out is dead."

That got me Prentice, something I ought to have seen coming. She wanted to know exactly how I knew what I had said I knew.

I took my time telling her about it, trying to pronounce everything clearly while she stared at my lips. "The girl who came here to pick me up for her mother is the daughter of the man who checked out Rose and Millie," I explained to Prentice. "He and his wife were separated but they were still married. No divorce."

Prentice nodded. "Go on."

"Naturally she and the daughter were notified when he passed away." I wondered whether Prentice was getting most of those words.

After a second or two, she said, "His heirs ought to return both the resources he borrowed."

I agreed and added that we could only hope they would do it.

"You know them. Will they?"

It's not easy for one of us to be deceptive; deception is something we rarely require. I said I doubted that they knew where he lived.

"Do you?" That was Prentice in a nutshell—no extra words.

I shook my head.

She turned, her slurred words drifting over her shoulder. "Come to my off'ce, Smit."

That sounded bad, but I had to do it. Like so many deaf people she made a good deal of noise opening windows, shutting doors, and so on. When she had settled herself behind her desk, she said, "When a library resource like Millie or Rose is overdue, we send a card urging that it be returned. No doubt you know."

I seated myself on her desk and nodded.

"That is what we did in this case. Our card came back marked 'deceased.' Does that surprise you?"

I shook my head.

"You didn't see that patron die, did you?"

I admitted that I had not, adding that I had spoken to his daughter and his widow and felt quite certain that he was in fact dead.

"I don't suppose you know Charlotte Lang."

The name rang a bell. After a moment I said, "I've met her. I don't know her well."

"She is a volunteer here at the library. Was that how you came to meet her?"

I nodded.

"I might even call her an eager volunteer." Prentice smiled. "Am I speaking well, Smit? Can you understand me, provided you concentrate?"

I nodded. "You are actually speaking quite clearly."

"Few of our volunteers can be called dedicated, yet it seems that Ms. Lang is. She has offered to try to locate the missing resources for us."

I nodded again. "You accepted?"

"I did. She asked then whether we had a disk or cube, or even a book, that might be of help to her."

I didn't mean to sigh, but I did it anyway. I thought it was easy to see where this was going.

"I was able to direct her to a book. You look surprised, Smit."

I said, "That's because I am."

"*Investigation for Amateurs* is the book. Perhaps you know it?"

I shook my head.

"I have not read it, but I wished to be helpful and could think of only one thing better. I also directed her to you. I feel sure you must be pleased."

I lied manfully.

"You are not familiar with the book?"

I said, "Correct."

"It would be well if you could look into it now. Unfortunately she has yet to return it."

I said, "Perhaps I'll be able to look into it when Ms. Lang checks me out."

Prentice nodded. "My thought exactly. You are very fortunate, Smit. Rarely is any resource in this library so fortunate."

Back on my shelf, I found that I could not read, study the patrons, or even reminisce; all those much-loved idle resources were denied me. I could only wait for Charlotte Lang now. Nothing else.

18

Buck Baston

H owdy!" the tall man who had stopped at my shelf said. He had a good voice and a better grin, so I smiled and said, "Doing pretty well so far. How about you?"

"Got taken out yesterday."

I had figured him for a patron; I tried to readjust my thinking.

"Don't reckon we've met up." He offered a sun-browned hand. "Name's Baston."

We shook; his hand was callused and somewhat larger than mine. Stronger, too. "Smithe," I told him. "Ern Smithe."

He cleared his throat. "Pleased. I hail from Westerns an' don't git over this way much. Reckon it shows."

"I don't believe I've ever been to your section of the library either, Mr. Baston. My loss, I'm sure."

"You git checked out more'n most. I flat out admire that, Mr. Smithe."

Something was up, but at the moment I had no idea what it might be. I said, "Not as much as I'd like, Mr. Baston."

"That's good." Baston paused. "I'm a resource myself, same as you. Born in Texas and growed up on a ranch. You had me figured straight off, didn't you?"

It seemed safe to nod, so I did.

"Same here, only I got checked out 'bout a week ago an' I'm gittin' renewed right this minute. Same lady."

I waited.

"This next is hard, 'cause I don't want you to git the wrong notion. I ain't puffin' up, jest tellin' the truth." He hesitated. "You kin call me Buck. I ain't one to stand on church-day manners all week."

I gave him the best smile I could manage. "Nor am I, Buck. Call me Ern."

"Ern? I never heard that 'un." Buck paused. "Know what it means?"

"Yes. It's *eagle*."

"Like to a Injun name?"

I nodded. "I'm afraid so."

"Then that right there's a name I'd be proud to bear. Not that I ain't proud of the one I got, only my friends mostly sez Buck." Buck Baston hesitated. "All right if I say Ern? Seems like we might be pullin' in the same team."

That sounded odd and interesting. I said, "You're being checked out again, you say."

"An' where's your patron? Ain't that the rest of it, Ern?"

"A fraction of the rest." I grinned and added, "I'll concede that."

"Nice watch you got there. What time's it say?"

I glanced at it. "A quarter to ten."

"She's goin' to meet us up front. Ten sharp she said, only she's got errands to run. That's what she called it. Errands. Reckon she might be beforehand. Think we might set out front an' keep a lookout?"

I said, "They'll want us to go back to our shelves."

Buck Baston grinned. "You ever see the big dictionary, Ern?"

"The one on the reading stand?"

He nodded. "Been there nigh on to forty years they say. Takes two jest to turn a page. They don't like it there, only three of 'em tried an' couldn't even close it. They give up after that is what I heard."

When I said nothing, he added, "I'm the same way." Abruptly his right hand held a gun. He spun it and returned it to a tooled leather holster under his jacket almost as swiftly as he had drawn it. If the librarians at the desk had seen it, they gave no sign.

There were two long benches in the lobby as well as a scattering of plain ponticwood chairs. When we had settled ourselves on one of the benches, I asked his patron's name.

"She's Miz Harper Heath. Ain't you wonderin' 'bout my gun?"

I admitted I was, and asked whether his patron knew he had it.

He chuckled softly. "She knows an' this library don't. She give it to me, bullets too. You want one? Have your own gun?"

"Perhaps. I'll let her know when I know what she wants me for."

"Haunts, I call 'em."

"Ghosts? Are you serious?" I was afraid I had not misunderstood.

"I've shot a couple. Bullet goes clean through an' into the wall." Baston paused. "The girl does it, is what I figure. That girl's brought 'em along, only she didn't know. Still don't, is what she claims. Won't believe it."

I waited.

"Reckon you're puzzlin' what all this has got to do with you."

I nodded. "Wondering, and hoping you'll enlighten me soon, Buck."

"That there's the girl's doin', too. I told Miz Heath to shy off from you, 'cause of that." Baston sighed. "She didn't pay no heed. Might as well tell you now. You're certain sure to find out 'fore much longer."

I said, "Who is the girl you mentioned? Is she a fully human?"

"Tells everybody she is, only she don't have no paper. Miz Heath bought her from that big school back east, or that's what she tells. Says she used to belong to some doctor that was a teacher in there."

Memories swooped down at me like so many vultures. Mostly to myself I muttered, "Dr. Barry F. Fevre."

"That's the one. He's passed, is what I hear."

"Yes. He has."

"Probably they just found her settin' in his office, er somethin' like that, is what I figure."

"No doubt you're right. Is her name Ricci?"

Baston nodded. "Sure is. Reckon you know her."

"I do." I paused, remembering. "I comforted her once. Someone—it doesn't matter who—had spoken in a way that hurt her deeply. I tried . . ." I paused again. "Well, I'm glad she hasn't forgotten me."

My new patron, Ms. Harper Heath, returned. We followed her out of the library, and Baston opened the door of her sleek silver flitter and helped her in. To my surprise, she patted the seat beside her own, saying, "Sit with me, Smithe. I need to talk to you and ask some questions, and this will be a good time to do both."

More than a little apprehensive, I walked around to the other side, opened the curved, tight-fitting door there, and somewhat clumsily climbed in. When the flitter was well above a sunlit sea of cloud, Ms. Heath asked, "What do you know of the occult, Smithe?"

I was tempted to say only that it didn't exist, but it seemed clear that would be imprudent. In place of it I put, "No more than the average person, I'm sure. Possibly less." Eager to enlist an ally, I turned in my seat to glance back at Baston. "What about you, Buck? Are you well acquainted with the occult?"

Silently, he shrugged and shook his head.

"Yet a librarian recommended both of you." The flitter rose, shoving us back in our seats while our patron spoke.

Stubbornly, Baston shook his head again.

"Do you insist that you have had no experience with the supernatural, Mr. Smithe?"

I said, "I do," making it as strong as I could. "Ricci and I met briefly in the ice caves of Lichholm. She's not exactly a friend, though I wouldn't call her an enemy. I take it you know about Lichholm? The island of Lichholm?"

"Only that a Dr. Fevre was doing research there. Is it nice?"

I shook my head. "No, it isn't, and I haven't the slightest desire to go back there."

Baston put in, "Ice caves don't sound like someplace a man would hanker to bunk at."

"Apparently Dr. Fevre took this Ricci girl off the island. If what you say is true, I applaud him for it."

Picking up speed, our flitter laid back its wings.

19

At Home with the Heaths

"Our home is what's called a progressive purlieu," Ms. Heath explained. Her voice was warm with pride. "It grows as our income increases. Last year there was no billiard room, for example. We live in a living thing, but not as parasites. We feed, protect, and groom it."

Like living inside a tree, I thought; but it seemed best to keep the thought to myself. That thought had waked a dozen memories.

"Your place will be in the library, Ern Smithe. Baston's already familiar with every room of it and can explain their features."

"It's lovely," I said, still looking at the house. "A beautiful home, and an imposing one."

"Thank you!" Ms. Heath sounded as though she meant it. "Have you ever been to Venice?"

I shook my head. "I'm afraid not. I can only hope to tour Italy someday."

"Long, long ago they built palaces on water there. Most have washed away now, but a few of the best have been documented and preserved. We recommended the plan and general appearance of those palaces to our own program here." For a second or two Ms. Heath paused, hesitating (I suppose) to explain something I might be familiar with already. "One can do that. Make constructive suggestions, whether the buildings you recommend are castles or cottages."

Baston nudged me. "You git her to show you the big ballroom, Smithe. Forty acres I trow if it's bigger'n my neck rag."

The flitter dropped alarmingly, then scooted toward the gaping roof of a hangar. As it settled to the hangar's smooth metal floor, I tried to digest the brief glimpse of the house our flight had given me, all the sharp roof peaks and wide domes, the glittering towers with airy turrets planted in rose-rich gardens.

Baston and I got out; the flitter lifted off at once, folded back dark wings, and was gone.

"This here house," Baston explained when we had left the hangar, "keeps on buildin' itself so long as folks live on the inside."

I asked how fast it built.

"Depends on how much money they give it. It's gotta eat. Gotta buy groceries. That's lumber, nails, bricks, plumbing an' all the rest, same as a contractor would. After that, it depends on the size. The bigger it is already, the faster it kin build more. It's a real big 'un now, an' can put on two little rooms per one day. Two littles or one big. What we're seein' now"—he waved at the house—"is a pretty fair size already."

It certainly was. I nodded.

"A' course funny wants kin slow the buildin' down some. Damage, the same. It fixes itself then 'stead of buildin' new."

I ventured that it sounded like magic.

"I s'pose, only it ain't real magic, you know. By an' by you an' me had best have us a little talk 'bout the real thing."

"Also ghosts, apparently," I said.

"We kin talk 'bout them soon as you've seen a couple." Baston paused. "Seein' helps make everthin' clear. That's ghosts an' money both."

At the front of the house, Baston spoke to the wide door, which swung back silently at once. "Didn't welcome us," he remarked to me.

I nodded. "Yes, I noticed."

"If we'd of had a fully human with us, somebody like Miz Heath, we'd of had that. It knows." Under his breath Baston added, "A fully human—or big money."

I cleared my throat. "Perhaps we should go into the room in which ghosts are most likely."

"While the sun's up, there's none likely." Baston's hoarse voice had fallen to a murmur. "Soon as sun's gone, everwhere's pretty likely."

I began exploring; Baston followed me, three or four steps behind. In a few minutes I found a capacious, square room whose only window was a wide skylight. Little tables flanked divans and comfortable-looking chairs. A large screen occupied one corner, a cold fireplace another.

I sat down to think.

Baston chose an outlandish loveseat built (or so it appeared) of horsehide, horns, and antlers. "You figure to wait fer the ghosts here?"

"Yes, and to get something to eat, if I may." I told the screen to show me the sun and the horizon below it. As I had expected, sunset was very near.

216 • GENE WOLFE

"You reckon you could order me something while you're set-tin' there, Ern?"

"Probably." I nodded. "What would you like?"

"Whatever they got. I've et here afore, an' it's all been good."

The screen supplied a list of suggestions. I chose two more or less at random.

"Do you believe in ghosts?"

I shook my head just as Baston said, "Nope!"

That one syllable seemed to hang in the air until Baston muttered, "You ask me that?"

I shook my head again. "I did not. And you didn't ask me, either. The obvious answer is that the screen did, but the question seemed to come from behind me."

"Well, I never did think it was you, not you nor that screen neither. There's devilment after dark in this here house. We jest got our first taste."

It seemed to me then that the room was growing darker, not because its lights were going out, but because a dark miasma had invaded its air. I managed, "What do they want?" without sounding quite as frightened as I felt.

"Them ghosts?" Baston paused, stroking his chin. "I don't rightly know. They never say, or anyways not ter me. Mebbe they don't know neither."

I looked my next question.

"Well, they'd say so wouldn't they? Tell us we got ter git it for 'em. Or else say hand it over, if they thought we had it already."

"But Ms. Heath must think I have it, or know where it is. If she doesn't, why did she check me out?"

"Don't have to be that, Ern. Could be other reasons. Them

librarians got her to take you is what she said. Why'd she lie about that?"

I sighed. "I'm certain she did not. They thought I was a malcontent, I'm afraid. They wanted me out of their library."

"There's more, Ern. Who was it jest now that wanted ter know if you b'lieved in ghosts? You got any ideas?"

Having none, I shook my head.

"Then we got a couple possibles. First one's was it a ghost talkin'?" Baston fell silent, considering the chance of a talkative ghost. Then, "You buy that?"

"Not until all other possibilities are exhausted."

"Same here. Way I see it, it was most likely the house. It kin talk, an' look around inside itself too." Baston paused, looking thoughtful. "You buy into that one?"

I nodded. "That's the most probable explanation I'm sure, although it seems an unlikely question for a house to ask unless it is actually haunted." A new thought struck me. "Or it fears that it is, or may be."

Baston's eyes searched the room before he agreed.

"Who would be haunting it, Buck? Have you any idea?"

Silently, he watched me.

"How many men have you killed with those guns of yours?"

I had feared his anger, but the question seemed to have flattered him. "Fully humans, you mean? Why, nary a one. None yet."

"Men of any kind, including clones, reclones, and whatever else."

Baston shook his head. "That right there's a question I'd be a fool to answer. How 'bout you, Ern? Men, women, 'bots, babies, an' kids. How many you done fer?"

I said, "None, I hope."

"Ghosts don't track a man down anyhow is what I've heard. It's the house gits haunted, not the man."

I said, "Let's hope you're correct."

"Well sir, I believe I am. If it gits bad, there's ways ter lay 'em, too. Sometimes those works."

"But you don't know the rituals." I found that I was smiling. "Neither do I."

"We could put 'un together jest fer us, maybe."

I considered it. "Perhaps."

"Somebody done it once, didn't they? It's only weeds and winds come of theyselves."

I nodded. "Now that you've brought the matter up, I remember something about laying ghosts. The text spoke of bell, book, and candle."

"Think you could find us the right book? 'Cept for that, don't none of it sound hard."

"No, it doesn't. We would pronounce a blessing over all three, after choosing an appropriate book." I paused to consider; ritual would be necessary, though by no means difficult. "Then march three times around the house, while ringing the bell and reading suitable passages from the chosen book by the light of the candle."

"You going to do that?"

I shook my head. "In the first place, we don't have a candle, a handbell, or a suitable book. In the second—well, there are warnings against it. Casting out one set of spirits often results in their being replaced by another, generally worse. Wise men don't expel spirits unless they judge them to be both ill-intentioned and dangerous. Are these our hostess's problem?"

My question was answered not by Buck Baston but by a voice behind me. "Not at all. I am."

I turned to look over the back of my chair, and saw what I momentarily took to be a dead man alive.

He smiled. "This house belongs to me. Although I did not invite you, you are entirely welcome here—at least until morning."

With more presence of mind than I had just then, Baston drawled, "Miz Heath, she'll have somethin' to say. She thinks it's hers."

"She is mistaken, though I don't argue the matter with her."

I thought I had found my mental feet by then. I said, "I saw them carrying out your body . . . Doctor." I was trying not to gulp. "Carrying your corpse." I hesitated, and at last added, "You were dead."

The smile widened. "I missed that spectacle. What was the cause of my death?"

"An arrow." I pointed toward my neck.

"Ah! Savages! Mr. Baston here must be delighted."

Behind me, Baston said, "I don't go lookin' fer trouble with 'em."

"Wise man! Certainly wiser than the fool—"

The speaker was interrupted by the arrival of our food. He sniffed, then inspected it.

I said, "I can order something for you, if you like."

"I would. Salmon, if the house still has it. Spinach and brown rice."

I ordered, and he thanked me. "I want to get to the bottom of this haunted house nonsense, but my brother's murder comes first. I'm sure you understand."

That caught me off guard. I stared until Baston muttered that we did.

"Did my poor niece weep?"

"Yes." I paused. "May I bring her in? She deserves to see that though your brother—is that correct? That although her father no longer walks among us, her uncle is still alive."

"In a moment; and I am also alive, just as she is. Not still alive since I was not expected to die. Please order my supper."

I explained that I had done that already, all the while listening to Baston's hoarse chuckle. Being dead, this new Dr. Fevre was telling him, gives one an appetite.

It took me about five minutes to figure out how he had managed to remain alive though his brother was dead; anyone who happens to read this lengthy account has probably gotten it already. Just in case you haven't, he had disappeared into this house, neither leaving it nor receiving visitors.

Baston stood and asked this new Fevre, "You want me to fetch Miz Heath?"

He shook his head. "She would surely feel that she was being treated like a servant in her own home. I'll have an opportunity to introduce myself soon enough, I'm sure. When I do, I must be prepared to talk to her. What difficulties does she face?"

"Ghosts, apparently," I said.

Fevre smiled. "Such as myself?" It was the smile of a parent told of some disagreement among his children.

I shrugged. "I wouldn't consider you a ghost, though perhaps she will."

He nodded thoughtfully. "No doubt the law would decide that I'm my own daughter's ward. Only too often, it does that sort of thing. Is my daughter here?"

"I'm told she is, but I haven't seen her."

"She may be shocked." Mr. Fevre paused to consider the matter. "We must minimize that if we can. I dare hope that—well . . ."

"I'm sure she'll be happy to see you." A new thought struck me. "I've been told that ghosts are occasionally mistaken for living human beings, particularly at night."

Mr. Fevre smiled as if quite genuinely amused. "How interesting! No doubt you also know the acid test used to distinguish between the living and the dead?"

I shook my head.

"A ghost may look and even feel quite solid, but a ghost cannot eat or drink. As soon as my salmon arrives, I shall be delighted to display my living humanity."

"We never figured you for no spook," Baston drawled. "Ain't that salmon going to get cooked in the kitchen, though? My vittles too, an' Ern's I guess. We countin' on Miz Heath to bring 'em out to us?"

Before Mr. Fevre or I could speak, Baston added, "She's off runnin' errands, is what she said. That grub's goin' to git cold afore she comes back."

A 'bot stepped into the room as he finished speaking. "I shall be delighted to serve you, sir. It is my office."

We asked it to serve our food as soon as it was ready, and busied ourselves rearranging furniture until the 'bot returned pushing a wheeled serving cart.

"You're a detective, ain't you?" Baston cut himself a piece of beefsteak. "What's Miz Heath want with you? You know that?"

"I'm not actually a detective," I explained, "just a writer who wrote books of the kind called mysteries. To populate my books,

I contrived a lovely young model forced by circumstance to become a detective, an alligator hunter who hunted criminals for whom the authorities offered rewards, and a criminal who helped the police in order to defer his own arrest. Now I assume that Ms. Heath wishes to talk about one of my books."

"What if she don't?"

Before I could reply, Ms. Heath herself entered the room. Baston and I rose.

20

Night and Day

Y ou haven't seen a ghost?"

For some moments the question hung in the air between us. Finally I said, "I don't think I have, although it's said that ghosts often pass as living persons. We were talking about that a few minutes before you came in."

"Do they really? I hope I never see it." Ms. Heath dropped onto a spindly-legged chair and motioned for us to take our own seats.

I sat. "Is that why you checked me out? To lay a ghost for you? There must be many people better qualified than I am. I've never done it, but I'll do my best if you want me to try."

"No, of course not. Do you know of anyone else in the library who has laid a ghost? Anybody at all? If you do—"

I shook my head. "No one."

"I checked you out to solve a mystery. Is that better? To protect me, too."

I said, "Buck here would be a better bodyguard, I feel sure."

"No doubt." Ms. Heath favored Baston with a quick smile.

"This gives me two of you, however. With both of you, I'm doubly protected—or so I hope. You haven't asked me about the mystery."

For half a second, I thought it over. "You'll tell me whether I ask or not."

"You're right. It's threefold, if you'll allow that. First, what is the treasure hidden here?"

Baston leaned forward. "There's treasure hid? Is this here real?"

Ms. Heath favored him with a wry smile. "It is said to be. I can't swear to it."

I asked, "Said to be by who?"

"The house." She sighed. "Don't try to cross-examine it. It doesn't know where the treasure is, or why it was hidden. There you have the second secret I spoke of, and the third. Presumably it once knew those things."

When neither Buck nor I spoke, she added, "Even human memories can be deleted; no doubt you know."

I nodded reluctantly.

"Inorganic memories are easier, though it's said that some-times a trace remains. I'm told that an expert might uncover it."

"I ain't one," Baston told her. "Neither's Ern, or that's my guess. Ern?"

I affirmed that he was correct, and asked why she had not called in an expert.

"It seems that all the experts are fully human. Are you aware of that? I looked high and low for one who wasn't, and was told over and over that there were none."

"No," I said, "I didn't know. What difference does that make?"

"A great deal. Their fees are—well, astronomical and far beyond my reach. I offered to share whatever they might find for me. I would take half and the expert half. My offer was declined." Ms. Heath held out her hands in an unmistakable gesture. "I won't offer you half, Mr. Smithe; but I'm making you the same offer I've already made Mr. Baston."

I turned to him. "Did you take it?"

He nodded. "Sure did."

"If we find the treasure," Ms. Heath continued, "I will lie to the library, saying that I've lost you both and so forfeiting both my deposits. You will live here with me, in whatever wing of this enormous house you choose. You will be free to come and go as you wish, and will receive any reasonable amount of spending money whenever you ask for it."

Baston and I stood when she rose.

"Meanwhile, you are to sleep here in the library," she told us, "although you are free to move about the house and grounds as you wish. Your sleeping shelves are in the third room."

When she had gone, I said, "High shelves, I bet."

"In this place," Baston muttered, "that there's the best kind there is."

He showed me the bathroom in which we could shower, and where I could change my clothes for a robe. I did so as soon as he left; naturally I hung on to my watch. Baston himself, I noticed, had retained his gun belt and both guns.

I seldom find it hard to sleep, but that night was an exception. I must have lain awake listening to the faint noises of the night for an hour or more. Eventually I clearly slept, for I woke to find myself walking toward a long, bare table ringed by eight chairs. To my left was a curved crystal wall, beyond that a rolling lawn dotted with pale groves and lit by moonlight.

For seconds that became minutes I stood staring at those groves before I set off in search of a door.

In a few minutes I discovered a narrow one hidden by a curtain. Something definite about the way that door closed and clicked behind me told me I was locked out. Tugging at the handle confirmed it.

In one way being locked out seemed serious; in another it did not. Serious because my patron was likely to think I had tried to run away. Not serious because it seemed to me that I was bound to find an unlocked door or an open window soon, given the size of the house, or that Baston might wake up and let me in.

Perhaps I ought to have tried to wake him by knocking on the door or tossing pebbles at windows. I did neither because the noise was liable to wake someone else, and it seemed to me that if I were to circle that enormous house I was sure to find some way to get inside. If I did, I was confident that I could locate the library. Turning to my left, I began looking for an unlocked door or window.

I hadn't gone far when I realized that a big dog, black or at least quite dark, was following me. I've always liked dogs; so I stopped, spoke to this one in a quiet voice, and let him sniff my fingers.

At that moment my watch struck one and the dog's ears went up. Softly I said, "That's just the little clock I wear on my wrist. It's called a watch, you see, but it strikes the hours."

The dog cocked his massive head.

"You ought to know all about those. I suppose you're a watch-dog yourself."

If the dog wagged his tail, it was too dark for me to see it. Reflecting that this dog was likely to be more intelligent than the dogs of my own time, and that talking calmly to a dog is generally a good way to show that you mean no harm, I said, "I'm locked out. Do you have a way to get back into the house?"

The dog appeared to nod, then turned and trotted away. I followed, walking fast to keep up. After two or three hundred strides we reached a wide porch, roofed, guarded with staunch pillars and furnished in shadows. I could just make out what appeared to be a narrow door on the other side. When I tried to open it, it would not budge. With a weary sigh, I looked down at the dog and was just in time to see his tail disappear.

Down on my hands and knees, I said softly, "Wuff!" all the while wondering whether the dog door had some way of distinguishing dogs from people. It seemed that it did not. I crawled through quickly and without much difficulty, watched by the dog. No doubt he was judging my dogginess and finding it less than satisfactory.

I have no idea what the occupants of the house called the room I had gotten into. There was a harp, stately and golden, with what seemed to be at least a hundred strings, all of which I was careful not to touch. There was also a painting (I could not see it clearly enough to judge whether it was finished) on an easel. Something in a cage snarled at the dog, then at me; its green eyes caught the light like emeralds. Twice life-sized, the statue of a bearded man with a woman's breasts bent to inspect me but offered no comment.

Very much afraid of being caught, I dodged around a flickering fire somewhere near the center of the room and found a new door. It was locked, or perhaps bolted on the other side. I was about to turn away when something poked the small of my back. "Reach fer the sky!"

I raised my hands. "Buck? Is that you?"

"Last time I looked." There was no more poking. "What the Sam Hill you doin' in here, Ern?"

I tried to explain.

"Well come on back 'fore somethin' worse than either of us gits us both." He led the way. "What you go off for? You dead set on getting burned 'fore your time?"

Using much too many words, I struggled to explain that I had walked in my sleep. When I had finished, Baston said, "You do that a lot, Ern? Goin' round like a spook?"

"No." I shook my head. "Never before, I think."

"Somethin' got hold of you then. You know what it was?"

I shook my head. "Nothing, I think. People do walk in their sleep sometimes."

"Could be somethin' gits hold of them, too. You sure you wasn't lookin' fer the treasure?"

"Perhaps I was." I shrugged. "I don't know."

When I got back on my shelf I couldn't sleep for an hour and more, and all sorts of thoughts flitted through my mind. At last I slept, and sleeping saw the fire. I was old and stooped and worn, the aged edition of myself who had stolen a scalpel from Dr. Fevre and taken his own life with it in the Polly's Cove Library. I was drawn to this aged self, as an iron filing to a magnet— then a woman's hand, hard and muscular but quite definitely a woman's, drew me back. I woke drenched with sweat.

Perhaps I slept again, though I doubt it; when I heard some-one walking in another room, I left my shelf. Shaved, after-shaved, and dressed, I waited in the kitchen for Ms. Harper Heath.

"Mr. Smithe! What are you doing up?"

"And off your shelf?" I smiled. "That's something else you'll soon ask. I thought I might save you the trouble. Will you talk to me while you have breakfast?"

"Listen to you, you mean." She paused, her head tilted left. "If you're going to tell me you've already found the treasure, I certainly will. Is that it?"

"I'm afraid not. I only want to offer a suggestion."

"Have you eaten?"

I shook my head. "I'm afraid not."

"You're repeating yourself. Sit down and order something. Whatever you want."

I did, ordering oatmeal and coffee.

"Were you tempted to order kippers, Mr. Smithe?"

"No. Kippers never occurred to me."

"Well, I'm going to have some anyway. I'll give you a taste when you've finished your oatmeal. Is that what you wanted? A taste of whatever I have for breakfast?"

I shook my head. "As I said, I want to offer a suggestion. I've been thinking about the treasure you mentioned, a treasure hidden here in the house, or perhaps buried on the grounds. It could be buried on the grounds, couldn't it?"

"Yes, as far as I know."

"That's what I thought. Buried treasure has usually been buried by pirates—in books, at least."

For a moment Ms. Heath stared at me, a small piece of kippered herring waiting on her fork. "Are you suggesting this one was? That's crazy."

"No, I'm not. I have no idea who may have buried it, or why. Do you?"

She shook her head. "None. The house says it exists, but that all further information has been deleted from its memory. I'm rich already, but . . ."

"Indeed. If you had more money, you might buy Baston and me from the library."

"And let you come and go as you please, with spending money. We've already been over that."

"It costs you nothing to check one of us out of the library."

Slowly, Ms. Heath nodded.

"You have to put up a big deposit, but it's returned when you return the resource."

"That's right. What are you getting at?"

Here it was. It might be a tough sell, but I was determined to make it. "I have a suggestion. I suggest that we bring in a resource I know who was once captured and held for ransom by pirates."

"And you think this man might . . ."

I was shaking my head. "She's a woman, and a very shrewd one."

"Is this somebody I've heard of?" Ms. Heath sounded interested.

"Very possibly. She's written a number of books. Her byline is Audrey Hopkins—Captain Audrey Hopkins."

The upshot was that Ms. Heath, Baston, and I went to the public library together. Audrey had been checked out, but Ms. Heath reserved her.

Baston sat up front beside Ms. Heath on the way back. From time to time one of them spoke. It may well be that I seemed to ignore some remark addressed to me. The truth was that I was so absorbed in my own thoughts that I paid little attention to what they said or the route of our groundcar. I had known women prior to Audrey and, while I was with her, assumed that I would know others after she and I parted. Now I could only long for her and weave plots that might reunite us.

As soon as Baston and I were back at the house and alone, I motioned for him to follow me and led him to a picnic table outside. "You got somethin'," he declared. "Somethin' you don't want that there house to hear 'bout."

I shook my head. "I only hope to get something. Do I have to tell you why I tried to get Ms. Heath to check out Audrey?"

He grinned. "Not less you want to."

"Then we'll skip that. Suppose we find the treasure. Will Ms. Heath keep her promise?"

"You're a mite smarter 'n that, Ern."

"Smart enough to value your opinion. Will she?"

"Depends on what it is." Baston drew one of his guns, thumbed the hammer back to half cock, and thoughtfully spun the cylinder. "If it's good, I won't have to use this. If it ain't, why I jest might."

"They'll burn you for it."

He shrugged. "Ever been to the Badlands, Ern?"

"Are they real? They sound legendary."

"A man could hide out there fer years if a hundred men was lookin' fer him. You an' me will have a talk 'bout them some other time, mebbe. You goin' back to bed?"

I shook my head. "I wouldn't sleep."

"Me neither. Sun'll be up in a hour or so. Lord knows I ain't the sharpest knife in the drawer, but I kin find us that kitchen."

21

A New Fevre

There was a table there at which a familiar figure sat. I smiled, pulled out a chair, and sat down beside her. "Good morning, Rose. Do you know who I am?"

For a long moment she stared at me, then favored me with a radiant smile. As she did Buck Baston joined us, sitting on my left. I nodded. "Yes, I am the copy of Ern A. Smithe who rode in the trailer with you and Millie. That copy of Ern A. Smithe."

She thanked me.

"Tell me something, Ern. . . ." Thoughtfully, Rose paused. "I . . . I'm not entirely ignorant but I need a lot more experience."

"What is it that you need to know?"

"I—well, am I right when I think that I'm fully human?"

"I'm afraid not."

"While you . . . ?"

Before I could speak, Dr. Fevre joined us, setting a steaming cup on the table and pulling out a chair.

I said, "I'm a reclone, Rose. So are you. I am a resource currently on loan from the Spice Grove Public Library. Dr. Fevre's wife checked me out of the Polly's Cove Public Library some time ago. In a few days I'll be overdue."

"I see. . . ."

"When I am it will be my duty to go back there if I can, and I'd like your help with that."

Slowly Rose nodded.

"May I have it? Have your help?"

She looked thoughtful. "Dr. Fevre checked me out. Would you like him to check you out too, or are you hoping he'll return you?"

Dr. Fevre smiled but said nothing.

"I'd like him to check me out, of course. That would give me three checkouts this year. I should be safe for quite a while."

Rose nodded, a little sadly. "I am already, Ern. Of course I'm the most recent edition at present. I . . . we romances age horribly fast."

"That can't be pleasant." I tried to make it as sympathetic as I felt.

"Sometimes I look forward to it, daydream about the peace and the quiet." One lily-white hand rose to cover her décolletage. "A whole year on the shelf when there's not one lonely man anywhere who wants to run his poor damp hands over everything."

Baston muttered, "Copper'd sooner be gold, only gold 'ud sooner be copper, passin' from one to the next 'un an' seein' the world."

"To remain on the shelf year after year, of no use to oneself or anyone else, is at least as painful as the fire," I told Rose. "One eats and sleeps, and watches impatient patrons in search of something one can only guess at. We call it gathering dust."

"And after that . . ."

I nodded.

Dr. Fevre had been listening. Now he went to the screen and gave his name. "My wife has checked out a resource titled Ern A. Smithe. My wife's name is Adah Fevre." He spelled it. "Smithe is here with me, and tells me he'll be overdue soon. I'd like to check him out myself."

"Do you have a library card, sir?"

"I have a universal card." Dr. Fevre got out the platinum card and displayed it to the screen.

A moment later he turned back to me. "All right, you're set for two more weeks. What do you know about the treasure?"

"Only that we found it and you have it." Biting back half a dozen questions, I added, "I take it you want me to help you figure it out."

"I want you to find out what it does, and how it can be made to do it safely, either in my company or in my absence. When you do, you must return it to me, your patron, and tell me what you've learned. I promise that you'll be generously rewarded." Dr. Fevre paused. "More than enough to let you buy yourself out, if the treasure lives up to expectations."

I asked, "Is that legal? Buying myself out? I've never even heard of it."

"That's because it's so rare. You need the help of a fully human who will act as the buyer of record, first buying and then freeing you. It takes a good deal of money. If you have that much, fully human help is easily found."

Mostly to myself I said, "If the treasure's as valuable as you seem to think, I'll be able to buy myself out."

Dr. Fevre nodded. "You may, if your share is large enough."

"Even if it isn't . . ."

"Money is always useful. I have no doubt you'll find a use for it."

"I'm not actually afraid of being burned," I said. "Not for myself, at least. There's a lady who checks me out for one day each year. That should keep me alive for a good long time."

"You're probably right, if she's faithful and doesn't die herself." Rose looked up from her omelet. "I take it she's fully human?"

"Correct. Do you know about the treasure we found?"

She shook her head. "All I know is that you two got it. Have you figured it out yet? It sounds interesting."

"This house seems certain it's powerful," I explained, "but it doesn't know any more about it."

When I had finished, Rose shook Tabasco sauce on what remained of her omelet, dotting its yellow surface with splashes of scarlet. "You think it might be gold and gems."

I shook my head. "That would be nice, but it doesn't seem probable. Money seems almost as unlikely. It might really be a scientific secret."

"That wouldn't interest me, since I couldn't understand it. Could you?"

"Probably not. It would depend."

"I guess it always depends." Rose fell silent. When I offered no comment she said, "We traveled in that trailer together, Ern, and you never tried to climb into my bed. Not once. Are we friends?"

I was quiet for a moment, remembering. "We aren't close friends, Rose. But we certainly aren't enemies."

She chewed and swallowed. "Aren't you hungry? I think I can probably order something for you."

I shook my head.

"I was. When peace comes at last, it finds us with an empty stomach."

I said, "Please eat. Don't mind me."

For half a minute or so she did. Then, "Care to tell me how you got here, Ern?"

"If you wish. The doctor's wife checked me out. She wanted to consult me, but didn't want—just then—to leave her home. She sent Chandra to fetch me. I assume you know that the Fevres have a daughter?"

"Of course. I take it she's not here."

"Correct. She's at home with her mother as far as I know. With Dr. Fevre's wife, in other words. Did you know he was married?"

"Yes. She'll be shocked to find me alive." The thought made Rose smile.

"Perhaps not. My guess is it will depend on her cycle. Her emotions rise and fall. You must know about that."

Rose nodded. "So do yours and mine. It's true of everyone."

"Then let's say it's more marked—much more marked—in her than in most of us."

"I suppose." Thoughtfully, Rose paused. "I can only hope she'll be pleased."

22

UNBURIED TREASURE

When Audrey came in at last, she didn't remember me. "You look terribly disappointed Mr. . . ."

"Smithe." Devastated, I forced a smile. "That's Smithe, with a final E. I—we were lovers, Audrey. Another copy of you, of course. This lonely copy of me."

"You're not much taller than I am."

I made an effort to stand straighter. "Needlessly, I'll acknowledge that you're correct. I'm not. I won't force the matter, force in love is always pointless." I made myself draw a deep breath. "Once we stood together at the railing of the *Three Sisters* to look out at the sea. That was another copy of you, I realize; but this lonely copy of me. I love you still. If I were to meet a thousand copies of you, I might go mad for joy."

"You're sincere." Audrey sighed.

"If ever in my life I have been entirely, utterly, sincere, this is it. All my life, ever since I was published, I have dreaded the Fire. Now I dread losing you."

"To the flames."

I nodded.

"Death takes many forms, Mr. Smithe." Though she spoke to me, Audrey's gaze was fixed on the green box.

Thinking to safeguard both this Audrey and the box, I stood up. In that I was nearly too late. Audrey grasped it too; I had to snatch it from her.

I triumphed, and reality reeled.